I0718076

It's Called Disturbing

Buddy Roy Baldry

Copyright © 2018 by Buddy Roy Baldry

All rights reserved. No part of this publication may be reproduced, stored in a retrieval system or transmitted in any form or by any means – electronic, mechanical, photocopying, and recording or otherwise – without the prior written permission of the author, except for brief passages quoted by a reviewer in a newspaper of magazine. To perform any of the above is an infringement of copyright law.

2nd Edition

Published by: Dimensionfold Publishing

ISBN: 978-1-9990694-6-9

Edited by: Danica Baldry & Ken Goudsward

Design and layout by Ryan Van Bavel

Author photo by: Susan Parmar

This is a work of fiction. It's not real, so don't try to tell me you know someone just like one of the characters because I will call you a liar. Any resemblance to any person, living or dead, is entirely coincidental.

This book is dedicated to my Frogs and my JD Boy

As well to Master Emery

(Don't read it until you're 18)

Chapter 1

The combined weight of agents in Tom Ryder's office is 1782.53 kg. 1782.53 kg ÷ 18 agents = an average weight of 99.02944 kg. The largest agent weighed in at 140.6 kg, making him well above the average. His framed photo still decorates the Hall of Fame hall. The man sold a ton of insurance and his name is revered. He is retired now but if you look hard enough you can still see the imprints of his shoes in the carpets. The second to largest agent is Walter (call me Wally) Russ. His record is no less outstanding, but he is not retired. Walter weighs 138 kg and sells a vast number of policies. His picture hangs top heavy in the Agent-of-the-Month slot, which seems to be perpetually reserved for him.

Down the hall from Tom are two women (89 kg and 94 kg) and four men (120 kg, 108 kg, 113 kg, and 126 kg) He is sandwiched tightly between this weight. Through no fault of his own Tom cannot top 70 kg soaking wet, making him sadly below the company average. He knows there must be smaller people employed here but he has never met any of them. He imagines them in the cafeteria struggling to keep up.

Tom was never self-conscious of his weightlessness until he joined the ranks of Consumer Life. Board meetings were heavy with innuendo: "Not enough meat on this proposal," this fat man in a gold tie would say, only glancing at Tom. "There would never be enough in this portfolio should the client start eating away at his own reserve," a ball of pink flesh would moan out of the top of her sweater. All eyes would be on Tom. He would listen and try to nod. He would try to make it look like he knew what was happening while pushing his pathetic stomach out to substantial proportions. He avoided wearing black, which everyone knew was thinning. "Tom, can you give us the skinny on this prospect?" the manager would say, and Tom imagined snickers all around. Tom would reply: "I'll put some pressure on him."

"You can try."

Only Walter (Call me Wally) Russ speaks to all the new agents in the office. "I've often heard," he often says, "that u$ old timer$ $hould only advi$e you rookie$ once you've been here a full year. To me, that'$ bull$hit." Wally wants to help. He guides. He advises. He confuses. He meddles. He intrudes. He controls. He makes $74,500 per year without even getting out of bed in the morning. It is rumored the man grosses $650,000 in an average year. "You know how?" He asked Tom once. "Doing what you're doing right now. In the trenche$. Getting the dirt done. Doing the dirt." Tom was never sure what he was doing. But he did feel dirty. Sales seemed to be a tricky business and, after his first training session four weeks ago, Tom was thinking it was more trick than business.

Wally was the training facilitator. "Your potential client$ will alway$ talk themselve$ out of purcha$ing your product." He told Tom and another recruit. "They will think of every excu$e not to buy life in$urance; we can't afford it, maybe when the kid$ are older, my job ha$ in$urance coverage, whatever. The$e are called 'objection$'." Wally used air-quotes a lot. "Your job, a$ agent$ of Con$umer Life, i$ to 'overcome' the$e 'objection$' and thi$ can be difficult, but there i$ $kill involved. Which I will teach." He held up one sausage-like finger, "Fir$t, I will teach you 'word track$' which are phra$e$ and analogie$ to help them make the right deci$ion." Tom and the other recruit nodded. Wally continued with his finger still in the air as if checking for wind, "Never appeal to intellect or rational thought. Alway$ go for the emotion. You u$e analogie$ to $tart the client thinking of wor$t ca$e $cenario$. It'$ called 'di$turbing' the client. Now, my favourite analogy to u$e i$ the one I call the '$pare tire' analogy."

The 'spare tire' analogy went like this: *Let me ask you: you have a spare tire, don't you? You know, a spare tire. In your car? I'm betting you do. Sure, you do. It probably came with the car when you bought it. But have you ever had to use it? Have you even seen it? Would you know how to change the tire? Maybe. Maybe not. But it better be there, right? When it was needed. You depend on the spare tire being there, don't you? You wouldn't think of going on a long trip without it being there, right? You've got your family to think of, after all. Think about it. Dark night. Cold. Twenty-five below. Snowing. Flat tire. But you got the spare. Or do you? Maybe not. You asked yourself a month before you took this trip: why would you need this spare tire? Takes up space. Sell the spare tire, you thought to yourself. And now there you are. Wife in the seat beside you. Baby asleep in the back. The older one starting to cry softly. Scared. Car only has a quarter of a tank of gas. You could walk fifty miles back to the last gas station. Would it be open? Would the heater work if the car ran out of gas? You don't know. You would have to walk through the snow. Suit jacket and all, you rugged pioneer. Would your family freeze while you were gone? You're afraid no one would stop to help them. Then you're afraid someone would. After all, you never know who could be on these roads at night. Your family is helpless. Your family is in serious trouble. Who would have thought the spare tire could alleviate this much pain? After all, you don't even know what it looks like. You sold it, thinking you would never use it. Now look. Frozen stiff family. Frozen stiff father who never had the forethought of a spare tire. That's all life insurance is, my friend: a spare tire. You might never need it, but it sure as hell better be there when you do.*

"It'$ called di$turbing," Wally said, "and it work$. Learn it verbatim." It was disturbing, Tom thought as he stared at the inspirational posters hung on the wall above Wally's head. They were filled with good looking, well-toned men and women climbing mountains and riding bikes up mountains and sitting smiling at the top of mountains. Captions below these happy people read 'perseverance' and 'integrity' and 'attitude is everything'. The posters were meant to motivate, and in the corners of the room were security cameras that were meant to hold you to it.

$$$

The Consumer Life building was at the bottom of Ballast Avenue, a sagging street consisting of mostly financial offices, banks, and car parkades. Tom's office was on the top floor. His ceiling protected him from a 6,000 kg slab of concrete that held up the other occupant's Hummers, SUV's and four-wheel drives. Tom drove a Cobalt.

The large windows of the Consumer Life offices challenged the other windows on Ballast Ave. They reflected the sky. The windows opposite bow in deference and only reflect the street below. No one outside can see in past the formidable glass, but inside a person can look outside if they care to. The massive structure is a serious grey and the oppressive tone persists even at night. And there are 485 people swallowed up inside its belly. Agents, bankers, and accountants are like internal organs inside the giant whale, masticating clients, digesting personal information, regurgitating financial solutions. The janitors are like parasitic fish droning and feeding on the day's activities. The building, the convivial host, allows itself to be cleaned although it could crush these little, insignificant men. Security cameras like the ones on Tom's floor are strategically placed all over the building and if these mechanisms and the security guards themselves are the eyes and the ears of the building, it is generally felt by most that the insurance agents are the asshole. Of all the lawyers' and accountants' offices in the building, the Consumer Life offices were the least used by any walk-in traffic. Scorn, however real or imagined, was ignored by Consumer Life management. "These other 'experts' in this building," the rhetoric went, "spend their lifetime savings on school and building a practice. Your start-up fees are minimal compared to them. And in a year or two your earnings will be on par."

A hand-written sign in the coffee room read: "Last year I couldn't even spell financial advisor…Now I are one." Management were not amused and pressed for the joker. If they leaned on the culprit a little too heavily, no one commented.

It was true for Tom. There was a suspicious ease with which he had become such an apparently important apparatus in the financial world. With two weeks training and a multiple-choice exam, his name was printed prominently and thickly on a stiff business card. He had 500 of them to give away. He had an office and a mahogany desk he could barely see over. His name was stenciled high on the heavy door and then he was left alone in the room. "Good luck," they told him and glanced meaningfully at the phone.

That first day, one month ago, he hung his credentials on the wall: a photocopied Certificate of Completion with his name handwritten in the designated area. Below and to the right, the signature of the President of Consumer Life was stamped in black ink. That first day, squeezed between the offices of two senior agents, two industry heavies, he felt something he had never experienced before: calm. He felt secure. He felt optimistic. Perhaps this one thing he could do. There were four nearly blank walls and a large wooden door protecting him. They sheltered and hid him. And the only noise from the offices surrounding him was muffled, intense and quiet, as though someone was trying to move unyielding objects never meant to be moved.

The peace he felt quickly dissipated, however. The first month there was nothing much expected of him: get to know the lay of the land, so to speak. See how operations went, learn some basic sales skills, learn about life insurance products and solutions, commit to memory the various analogies meant to motivate people to protect themselves with life insurance. Get his feet wet making cold calls to total strangers. Learn to handle objections and rejections:

"I already have life insurance." And he would answer, "Yes but are you sure there is enough coverage?"

"I have insurance through work." And he would counter with, "Fair enough, but should you get fired or leave the company, you would be much older and harder to insure."

"How did you get this number?" He would offer a guilty, "It's in the phonebook, sir."

"Why don't you piss off?!" He had no answer for the people that hung up before he could launch into his rehearsed spiel.

It was a small point of pride that both the other agents who were taken on at the same time as Tom were no longer there. It was only one month but he survived longer than two others. The first one to go lasted one hour and thirty-two minutes. He made it through orientation fine, but at the midway point in the initial training video, he stood up in the dark, blocking the projector with his body, said "Fuck this noise," and left. No one went after him.

The second new agent to leave was called David. During orientation David told Tom that he could tell right away they would be longtime friends. He told him within minutes of their meeting. They would be partners in this new gig called Consumer Life. They would take on the world of sales. Their pictures would sit side by side in the Hall of Fame hall. In a few years, they would be running this company. Maybe open a branch of their own somewhere. Maybe compete with Consumer Life eventually and corner the market. David pointed out all the things the company was doing wrong. He could tell the first day on the job that they were doing things ass-backward. During the first board meeting, David was going to tell the other agents the great ideas he had. They would be impressed, he was sure. And Tom could take credit for some of these ideas if he wanted. "That's ok," Tom said, and David winked.

It wasn't that the ideas he presented during the first board meeting he and Tom attended weren't good. It wasn't as though his ideas did not hold any water. The problem was David himself could not hold any water. All the heavyweights were there, and the managers stood in front of them introducing the new recruits. Tom nodded to the applause and the murmurs of welcome. David stood when introduced, and told everyone how happy he was to be a new member of the Consumer Life family.

When Stan the senior manager smiled, it took his whole face by surprise. His eyes wrinkled, and the corners of his mouth touched his ears. His hairline moved back ten years. "We heard you have some great plans for the office here, David." And then he indicated to David that he had the floor, even though David was already standing.

"You heard…? Plans?" Tom could tell David had lost some of the bravado he exhibited when they were in private and David was expounding on his ideas. His usual squared shoulders sagged a bit and he emitted a small, nervous laugh, "are the walls in my office bugged?"

Stan the senior manager's smile faltered, and he glanced over at Walter (Call Me Wally) who nodded once and said, "It'$ a joke." Stan the senior manager's smile returned, and he closed his eyes and held his head back and shook his shoulders twice. Tom assumed this was a laugh.

"Well, mostly just stuff I was thinking about, from my last place of employment." David spoke softer than Tom had heard him speak before. In their few encounters he was loud and liked to be loud about two inches from Tom's face. "I worked for a security company, selling security alarms…"

"Go on." Stan the senior manager coaxed.

Tom suddenly did not want David to 'go on' with whatever story he was going to tell. If it was the story he thought it was, then it was a bad idea. It was something David had told Tom and the other recruit (What the hell was his name? The 'fuck this noise' guy) sometime during their first few days. "This thing they call 'Disturbing The Clients?' It's nothing new, man." David had told them over coffee. "We used to do it all the time at the security company I worked for. You'd go to someone's door and tell them we were installing a security system across the street," He held up his hand to the side of his face pretending to whisper, "We weren't." He grinned. "But we would say we were installing this security system in their neighbourhood and would they be interested in checking it out for their own home. And sometimes that worked and sometimes no. But if they hesitated we would tell them about break-ins happening. The wife gets scared and they let us in and that's practically a sale. But the tough ones, the ones that say no thank you no matter what you tell them?" Here he leaned in close, but his voice was still loud, "We would give a kid, like, $50 to scope out the house and when they weren't home the kid would bust a window. Not go in or take anything, but just bust the window so it looked like someone broke in." He laughed, "Harmless, but it worked. The next time we came around the wifey would be drooling to sign a contract for the best security they could get. It's called disturbing the client. Same thing."

If this was what David was about to tell the management and agents at Consumer Life, Tom wanted no part of it. He shifted uncomfortably and tried to catch David's eye to tell him to shut up. But the managers were smiling and Stan the senior manager was smiling, and Wally was smiling. The other agents were staring down at blank notebooks. One of them sighed audibly.

"Go on." Stan the senior manager said again.

Fortunately, or unfortunately, David reached for his bottled water and swallowed three big swallows. "Well," He tried to clear his throat, but his face contorted and he dropped his chin giving it some impressive rolls. He began to cough silently, internally, then louder as his whole body rocked with convulsions. He put his hand to his chest and then outwards to the group, begging their pardon. He turned away and coughed. Soon his shoulders stopped moving and he turned back, red faced and trying to smile. Then the coughing started again. "I'm… sorry…" He was sputtering, "wrong hole…" The coughing and sputtering got worse and he placed both hands on the table in front of him and leaned over, "Son of a bitch!" He croaked loudly and everyone in the room began to rise from their seats to offer help or escape, Tom wasn't sure. "What the fuck?" David shouted and threw up a small stream of clear fluid on the table. He spit a few times and looked up at Stan the senior manager. "Wow." He tried to smile.

"Ok then." Stan the senior manager said as everyone stirred uncomfortably in their seats. "Why don't you step outside and walk it off."

"Wrong hole…" David said moving to the door and waving apologetically to the room.

"Of course." Stan the senior manager said and winced at the pool of bile on the boardroom table. "Let's call this a meeting and get to work, eh?" There was shuffling of papers and scraping of chairs as the agents rose to their feet.

Tom never saw David again. At the next meeting Stan the senior manager told the group that David had left to pursue other interests. "What can I $ay," Wally told Tom later in private, "He puked on our table."

Chapter 2

His commute home took him north away from the mid-city high-rises, through the business section and its three to ten storey buildings, winding him through the maze of split level homes in the suburbs, and back into the low rent district near another business centre: a valley of subway stations and basement suites. On his way, he drove over two rivers flowing South, eight railway tracks where at least one passenger train heading somewhere else made him wait, and underneath one airport runway. The planes never seemed to be landing. Always taking off.

His basement suite was located at the bottom of a cul-de-sac only a few blocks from the Trans-Canada. The upper floor was once a dance studio but now served as a quasi-warehouse for a clothing franchise and housed around a hundred naked, headless mannequins. There was a false front to make the building look like an actual house and from the street the deception was remarkable. When Tom parked his car and walked along the side to his entrance, the pretense of the siding disappeared. But the neighbourhood was quiet and the rent was cheap. He only had to forget that there were over a hundred decapitated nude mannequins, sans nipples, over his bed at night. Some tied to the ceiling. He imagined he could hear them twisting, floating and bobbing above him.

They didn't bother his girlfriend. "It's like… it's like they've been buried in a pit and we're underneath that, even. Like we're the worms." She said. Or: "It's like heaven, really. What you think is heaven turns out to be a nightmare. Or hell." Tom could only nod. She would take this as agreement or encouragement and continue on with darker analogies, but he only meant he heard.

No one seemed to ever collect or deliver the mannequins. They were just there. The image would not be so dramatic and unsettling if there were curtains on the windows, but the big bay windows showed the figures in his headlights as he arrived home at night. When he left for work in the morning they were there in his rear-view mirror. Headless. Soulless. Nipple-less. As he drove further away their images would disappear like something sinking in murky water.

$$$

When he got home there was no inviting smell of a roast in the oven, no beer waiting in a perspiring glass and no girlfriend gushing at his arrival. "Eddy?" He called. He set his shoes in the closet next to his other pair. He rolled up his sleeves. "Eddy?" Through the flimsy walls, he heard her tiny voice calling out over the sound of the shower.

He opened the refrigerator and watched the light dim and surge. There were three Schooners. He felt it might indeed be a three Schooner night. He twisted the cap off the beer. "Did you eat?" He shouted. He heard her diluted voice. Then the shower stopped. "How was work?"

"We were swamped," Eddy called back. She floated into the room naked, a towel wrapped around her sodden hair. She rubbed vigorously, her small breasts shaking, and let her black hair fall in waves, hiding her face. She saw him looking at her. "Don't, Tom. Stop."

"What?" He skipped the beer cap across the kitchen counter and it clanged into the sink.

"Stop." She said again and found a rag and wiped where the cap touched the counter tiles. "Jeez, Tom." She folded the rag and continued towelling her hair. "How was work?" He watched her walk down the hall to the bedroom. She took the towel from her head and covered her bottom. "Don't, Tom."

There was only one battery in the remote control and he tossed it beside him on the couch. Their basement suite was small;, one bedroom, one bath, kitchen and living room separated only by a half-wall. The furnishing cobbled together from their previous domiciles. The only art on the walls were Eddy's dark charcoal drawings and scratchings; images of stark trees, empty and abandoned buildings, and various depictions of people that, when you stood back far enough, were just skulls painted in a way that they resembled something else. The suite had windows that were all near the ceiling, the rest of the building being submerged in the earth. Soft yellow light from the sinking sun poured in and washed out the television screen.

He blinked at his reflection for a few minutes. "Did you eat?" He asked. He couldn't remember if he had asked her before.

She shuffled in and sat in the easy chair across from him. Her hair hung over her face, dripping tiny puddles in the shallow of her collarbone. Her hands clutched the inside of her sweater and her toes curled themselves inside the cuffs of her loose jeans. "How was traffic?" She said.

He shrugged. "It was an easy flow." He sipped his beer. "Did you eat?"

"Did you sell anything today?"

"Nah." He said. "Did you eat yet?"

"Yes, Tom." She sat forward suddenly. "I ate. I ate. I fucking gorged myself." She said, her handless arms bouncing up and down in a facsimile of violence against the chair. "That's all I did was eat all day."

"What the hell?"

"Are you happy? I heard you the first fifty times." She fell back and turned her head to focus on one of the plants. It was in sorry need of water. "I ate."

"Jeez, Eddy, I just want to know if I should fix us both something. Or if you were cooking, or what." He sipped his beer. It was empty. He placed the bottle on the coffee table and it made a hollow thump. A bubble formed at the top of the bottle and he poked it with his finger. There was silence between them.

Eddy sat curled on the chair as though she were trying to hide. "Sure, Tom." She said. Her face was flushed. How white she was against her clothes. Her hands and feet struggled in their prison, "We can have spaghetti."

"Spaghetti's fine." He said. Gently, appeasing. "You want me to boil the water?"

$$$

But first the bathroom. It was obsessive the way he would check. He was ashamed. How would he explain himself if she ever caught him? He performed his nightly secret ritual with the bathroom door locked and the sink water running. He lifted the bag from the garbage can. Slowly, slowly. The crinkling could be heard through the walls despite the running water. There was nothing underneath the bag in the container. He sniffed. It stunk like garbage. Good. Now the sink. The water ran and quickly drained. Nothing clogged down the sink. Good.

The mirror was hinged in the middle, halving his face. Inside the cabinet bottles and vials lined the shelves from smallest to largest. Eight different brands of headache relief. 50 Tabs APO Prednisone 50 Mg. Take as directed. Celesoderm Val.0.1% CR. Apply sparingly to affected area(s) twice a day. Venlafaxine XR 150Mg. Effexor XR 150Mg. Take ONE capsule(s) daily. Take With Food. Good.

A sharp knock at the door made his heart do an excited flip. "Tommy, hurry up. I have to do my hair." He heard Eddy from behind the locked door.

"I'm almost done." He said, too loud. Did that sound unnatural? Would she suspect he was snooping through her things for evidence?

"Well, don't stink the place up."

Shit. Of course. It dawned on him quickly and sent a tingle through his scalp. Why hadn't he thought of that earlier? Days ago? He opened the small cupboard below the sink. He moved the rolls of toilet paper and a box of tampons. And there it was; one box of Ex-Lax. Opened. He looked to the toilet. Slowly he pulled the seat up and bent to look inside. The water in the bowl was clean. He flushed. And there, just underneath the rim. He knew it. He leaned closer, resisting the urge to investigate with his fingers. She had cleaned but not enough. There were tell-tale splatter marks.

$$$

At night the reflections from Eddy's fish tank played across their bedroom like a visible aquamarine breeze. Tom stared at the ceiling and imagined the mannequins just above this surface, bobbing and swaying. Each time he closed his eyes they stayed shut a little longer. When he opened them the shadows were further away and he felt as though the ceiling was slowly receding from his view. Eddy rolled to her side facing away from him. Her movements made the waterbed pulse and roll beneath his back. In his ears, the silence was threatening. No longer simply quiet but oppressive, coming from inside his head, as if his ears were blocked or plugged. He closed his mouth and blew gently through his nose. Nothing. It still felt as though he had been swimming. He stuck his fingers in his ears and wiggled. "Hello? Hello?" His voice was far away.

"What?" Eddy beside him. Groggy.

"Nothing." He said. "Sorry."

"What?"

"I feel sick." He said. Now it was difficult to breathe. Each word he said expended precious energy and air. His heartbeat played catch up with his lungs. He could not get enough breath.

"Welcome to my world." She said.

Indeed.

Our world, she meant. Her world no longer existed. His own world no longer existed. It was a mixture. They had taken their individual colours; beautiful yellow and a sublime orange and created a… what? She would know the colour. To him it resembled puke. The colours would never disassemble again. The two of them together were a new entity. Not an entirely useful or pleasing one. Much like the septic pond behind his parent's farm; N parts water, N parts shit. The shit to water ratio was unknown. Besides, who would dig and wade through all that green swamp to find out. This is how he thought of his relationship when he was just about to fall asleep. His subconscious would clamour for attention as he drifted off. Work was wrong, he and Eddy were wrong, this basement suite was wrong… it all seemed wrong.

After a minute he knew she was sleeping again. He concentrated on the ceiling and on the headlights that swept past the window, whitewashing the room, as a lighthouse would. He let his body float with the waterbed until his breathing slowed. And when he stopped struggling while drowning in doubt and indecision, there would come a peace. A calm. A letting go.

There. Nothing wrong. The day was an island disappearing over the edge of the world. The office was a bad thought. The other agents were sharks sinking down, nothing to feed from where Tom floated. The management whales were spouting off for no one. Certainly not for Tom's benefit or detriment. Floating the way he was, there was no sickness. He was all right. He could sail through this life. His basement suite could soon turn into a mortgage with a floating interest rate. Swilling drinks with the boys at the pub on Saturday. Wash the Cobalt (no, they could buy a luxury car) on Sundays. A calm ocean with his course directly in front of him. Why were things in his life never this clear in the morning? The stars so clear for navigation. The constellations plotting his actions. He should call his mother. Ease her mind. The job was fine. The job was fine. The job was fine.

And Eddy. Eddy.

He turned, letting the bed fool with his equilibrium. Letting the soft sheets fool with his libido. Eddy. He listened to her breath. Shallow. Like there was something up her nose. He pulled the blanket from her shoulder and admired the dark shadows in her collarbone. Such soft skin. He was attracted to her skin first, he remembered. Pale. When he first asked her out she reddened so quickly. Endearing. Just a film, he told her. Dinner? No, dinner was their fourth date. By then it was too late. He was in love. At least he thought he was, then. He traced lightly along her exposed ribs, feeling the defined grooves. The sharp bone of her hips gave his heart a pang.

"Tom, don't." She mumbled. "I'm fat."

Chapter 3

In the morning the car made a gurgling noise and refused to turn over, so Tom called a taxi. The traffic seemed heavy and the ride to work seemed slower. The leaden sky pressed down on the buildings which huddled together optimistically, putting on brave stone faces. The trees, wet with autumn, conceded their leaves. The leaves clung to the ground, trampled by pedestrians bundled in overcoats with their heads down, not wanting to admit to each other where they thought they were going. Probably they were not sure themselves. Tom was not sure.

The cab drove in a comfortable hum and concise corners. They passed a park Tom had never seen before. The street was not familiar. He shifted in his seat. Could this taxi be taking him on a longer route, to make his fare costlier? The ride passed from literal to figurative. He felt he was being taken for a ride. "Excuse me?" He said.

The driver was a pair of dark eyes in the rear-view mirror. "No problem." The driver said with a thick accent. "I get you there quicker. Sneaky back door."

"I don't need to get there quicker." Even ten minutes too soon to the office was an eternal wait. The second hand moving with a weight attached and the XII that signified lunch were roman numerals at the top of Mount Olympus, impossible for mortal minute hands to ascend. Tom did not need to be early for the morning meeting.

"Sneaky back door." The eyes said. "I know this city like…"
He held up his hand for Tom to inspect and verify. "Sneaky back
door."

The edge of the park slid by. Oak trees exploded colours into
the sky; reds and yellows rained down. "Beautiful time, eh?" The eyes
said. They shifted from Tom to the street and back.

"Sure," Tom said and closed his eyes. His head banged on the
side window as they raced over speed bumps.

"Not beautiful time?"

"Whatever, I don't know."

It began to rain. Droplets of water ran in streams down the
windows. Other car's wipers started up rapidly blinking away the rain.
Tom could hear the tire's whispering through the street. He could feel
a breeze on his neck. The driver's window was open a crack and rain
splattered in spitefully. The driver seemed not to notice. His eyes
focused more on Tom than on his blurred windshield. Tom turned
away to avoid eye contact. Billboards replaced the trees. Dancing cell
phones, giant clowns selling burgers, loans of cash that Tom
apparently already qualified for. Gentle nudges from a better life than
his.

"You are thinking about the ducks?" The driver's eyes said.

"The what?" Tom said absently, looking instead at the ribbons
of water running down the side of the window. Tom heard the driver
sigh heavily. The cab lurched to the right and off the busy street. Car

horns screamed, and the driver jabbed his middle finger in the air without ceremony. The car stopped underneath a large billboard advertising for an Optometrist's office: "We Help You Look Better." The sign read, and a large female face smiled down on him through the rain. Her ten-foot hand delicately held a pair of relatively small frames against her face. "See?" The image blurred as the wipers moaned and squeaked across the windshield. The driver turned in his seat to face Tom. He was smiling and tapped the side of his temple with one brown and crooked finger.

"You are thinking about the ducks." He said.

"What the fuck are you talking about?" Tom held out his hands, imploring the man to drive him to work. Around him, cars rushed north on the opposite side of the meridian, south on their side. Everyone was going to be on time except him. Early was bad; on time was OK. Late was uncomfortable. He fingered the warm vinyl of the door's armrest and found the handle.

"Do you know how long I drive cab for?" The man asked. Tom met his eyes. Uni-brow. Bad teeth. Very big smile. He looked at the meter. The red numbers clicked to $14.50. The driver reached behind absently and reset the numbers to zero. "You don't worry about that, no sir. You know for how long I have been driving a cab for?"

"I don't know." Tom winced and shook his head. "Since six o'clock?"

The driver frowned. Then smiled again. "Ha, ha, jokeyman. What is your name?"

“Tom?” There seemed to be no reason to lie.

“Belraj.” The man jerked a thumb at himself and then held out his hand as though to shake. Tom raised his hand in return and let it fall into his lap, realizing there was a plexiglass divider between them. The man was simply gesturing to better make his point. “I have been driving Taxicabs since 1978.” Tom nodded and feigned amazement. Speechlessness. He mouthed the word wow. “Uh-huh. Long time, eh? Long time.”

Through the windshield, over Belraj’s shoulder, the billboard’s image changed. The glasses on the woman’s face faded away and her eyes blinked once. After a few seconds, the glasses faded back into view. She blinked again. “We help you look better…See?”

“And do you know where I started driving the Taxi?”

“I haven’t got a clue. Look, could we…”

“New York City.” Belraj paused, letting this sink in. “It’s a very big town.” He smiled.

“I need to get to work,” Tom said finally. He leaned forward and touched the Plexiglas that separated them. Belraj slid the partition aside and gently touched Tom’s hands. Then, as though embarrassed, turned forward in his seat. He did not attempt to pull out into traffic, however. Tom shifted his buttocks around. “I am really going to be late.” When was the time to begin panicking? What was the protocol? Was there a necessary amount of pleading that would legitimize threats? Did pleading even have to preclude threats? Was it correct to ask for his cab number? Or license? The lack of etiquette criterion was crippling.

"Tom," Belraj said, "I drove Taxicabs in New York City for twelve years before I came to this country. Do you think twelve years in the Big Apple gave me some insight into human nature?"

"I would like you to start the car and drive me to work, please. Now."

"In my second year there I picked up a gentleman. He was a little chubby and he sweated. He wore glasses." Belraj gestured to the billboard. Eyes closing. Glasses appearing and disappearing. Ten-foot delicate fingers caressing the arms of the lenses. "He made me drive around Central Park seven times and kept asking me about the ducks."

"I will call your employer," Tom said. The woman in the billboard blinked languidly. What lovely fingers, he thought. French manicure. Why did he know this? Beautiful.

"'Where do the ducks go, Belraj?' He kept asking me, 'In the winter, what happens to the ducks?' And finally, I get angry and try to throw him out of my cab. He says, 'No, no. That is not the way. That is not how the book goes.'"

The eyes were not green. And not blue either. What was the colour for water? Marine? Aquamarine? Now the glasses were there but they did not mask the eyes the way Tom suspected they would. In fact, the eyes were enhanced. They glowed. Now the glasses evaporated. The slow liquid blink. Tom could still see the ocean eyes leaking between the drawn shades of eyelids.

"So, I see the book sitting next to this chubbyman. I don't know it then," Belraj tapped the side of his head. "But I know it now, oh boy. 'Catcher in the Rye' I read it many times after that."

"Catcher in the Rye?" Tom nodded. Sure. High school. Did anyone have eyes that colour in real life?

"That man is retracing the Catcher in the Rye's footsteps around New York City," Belraj said. "I had no idea at that time what was going on. What was going to happen."

In Tom, curiosity resembled anger. It was slow to build without true instigation. Self-righteous restraint could be a cousin to skepticism. But once piqued; once primed, both can evolve quickly. Both mutate and hunt for resolution. Tom's anger dissolved to curiosity this quickly. "That guy was in your cab?" He asked. "That Chapman guy? On the same day?"

"December the 8th, 1980." Belraj nodded solemnly. "He killed the Beatleman."

"That's something." Tom admitted. "like, THE Mark David Chapman."

"It is something. And I wonder what he is doing, acting out like a book. So I let him stay, thinking no harm will come to Belraj, and he asks me about the ducks and I tell him I do not know."

"And then?"

"And then he says: 'I need a hooker.'"

Tom formed the word wow. This time there was no irony in the facial expression.

"I drop him off and see him all over the newspapers and the televisions for the next many years." Belraj finished and breathed deeply, expelling the memory, expelling the actual deed. "And when I see you today…" He waved off their meeting, turning to the traffic passing them by. "In my taxi, I come across someone every few years who does not like to see the leaves falling from the trees. I see it in their eyes and in the way they answer my queries."

I don't know what you mean Tom wanted to say. But he felt his eyes pulled upward. Two small bubbles rising quickly to the surface of a dark sea. The woman in the mural magically replaced her glasses and blinked at him. Winked at him. Her face looked so smooth. Clean. Soft. Fleshy and round. The only sharp angles were cheekbones.

Belraj turned to face him straight on. "My friend," he said slowly while Tom looked everywhere but in the man's eyes. "Speak to someone you love. You are drowning."

Tom snorted scorn. In the rearview mirror, the morning heat shimmered and distorted the image of oncoming cars. Their bodies floating on invisible waves, tires appearing like landing gear on floatplanes. Over Belraj's shoulder, the office towers sat fat and wide, the upper stories trying to block out the sun and snag the clouds. They were the large black rocks on a foreboding island. But above their shared life raft Belraj and Tom both stared at the wondrous siren that guided them to a safe oasis.

Belraj jerked his thumb at her image. "I love women with glasses." He leered. "You take them off you got a different chick."

This made Tom laugh, knowing how much Eddy would disapprove of the word "chick", but hell, this was just two guys sharing a private joke. Two warm-blooded men looking at a photo of a beautiful woman. Two men of different generations, enjoying... Tom frowned. What year did Belraj say he drove taxi in New York City? 1978? Tom counted backwards in his head, lost count and began adding decades to the year 1978. How many years was that? That couldn't be right. "Hold on a second, Belraj," Tom said as the cab moved slowly back into the morning traffic.

"I told you, Tom, no worries, you won't be late my friend."

"How old are you?" Tom asked, sitting forward to get a better look at Belraj in the rearview mirror. "How old did you say you were again?" The eyes looked back at him, suddenly shifting from the street ahead to Tom, they creased at the corners as if Belraj was smiling. But Tom could see a small bead of sweat appear on the man's dark forehead. "You drove cab in 1978?" Tom asked. "What were you? Ten years old?"

"Pshht.." Belraj waved a hand in the air and changed lanes too quickly, causing a cacophony of horns. He gave a nervous laugh. "Sneaky back door."

"You didn't drive cab in New York City, did you?" Tom asked. No response. "You didn't meet that man that killed Paul

McCartney at all, did you?" Tom was leaning forward in his seat now, trying to meet the man's shifting eyes.

"Not Paul McCartney, he died in a car crash in 1966." Belraj said, the thick accent suddenly gone. A Canadian East Coast twang Tom heard now and then around the city. "You're thinking of John Lennon."

"What the hell, man?" Tom said, genuinely offended. "Why would you lie about that?"

"Hey, man, give me a break," Belraj said. Tom was looking at him closely. He seemed now much younger than his previous accent suggested. "I'm studying to be an actor. Just trying things out on you. Pretty good, eh?"

"So that didn't happen?" Tom asked.

Belraj wrinkled his brows as he glanced back at Tom. "Come on, dude, I bet we're the same age. I was just trying out a character. Channelling my grandfather or something."

"But you made up that whole story!" Tom was agitated now.

"Oh, come on!" Belraj twanged, "I was just trying something out. Plus, those conspiracy stories kind of give me a kick."

Tom slumped back in his seat, disillusioned. "Huh."

"Oh, don't flip out," Belraj said and pulled the car to Tom's building, double parking. The meter still read $0.00. "Everyone is obsessed with something."

Chapter 4

The water cooler went glug, glug, glug, with a weighty authority. Nearly empty, but the bottles sitting full on the floor appeared too heavy for anyone to bother replacing.

"Did you hear about this salesman guy that died and went up to heaven?"

"Yeah?"

"Anyway, this insurance guy dies and goes up to heaven and St. Peter's about to let him in the gates, you know, with full benefits and everything…"

"Full benefits, hah!"

"Yeah, but there's the Devil standing there and he says to this insurance guy, 'Hey, man, don't go in there until you check out what I have to offer.'"

"Yeah?"

"No, wait. First of all, Peter says to the guy, well, you aren't good and you aren't bad you could either go in here or down below, you know."

"Right… heh…"

"Right, and the guy says, you know, no contest, I'll go in here."

"Full benefits."

"With full benefits. And then the devil tempts him down. So the guy figures, what the hell, it's not like he can keep me there, right?"

"Right…"

"Right. So the guy goes down below with the devil and, wow, the place is incredible. This beautiful blonde meets him at the door. And there's tennis courts and Jacuzzi's, and the devil shows him his house that he would live in and it's, like, a mansion…"

"Heh… heh…"

"And the devil tells the guy that this is just the beginning…"

"It gets better, eh?"

"It gets better all the time. Anything he needs, he can get it (snap) just like that. And the guy, he's all, 'Oh, wow!' And the devil lights him up a big cigar and gives him a big glass of wine and the beautiful blonde starts rubbing his shoulders and coming on real lovey-dovey."

"Heh… heh…"

"And the guy says: 'sold' and he signs the contract and heads back upstairs to tell Peter that there's been a change of plans."

"No doubt… heh… heh…"

"And he heads back down to start living the high life. But when he gets there, things have changed."

"Uh, oh… heh… heh…"

"Yeah, things have changed, all right. Now it's all fire and brimstone and crap, and much gnashing of teeth. And the guy says to the devil: 'Hey, what the hell? I thought this place was paradise, you told me things were going to be real good down here.' And the devil says back to him: 'Oh, right. Well, that was when I was recruiting…"

"…"

"That was when I was recruiting…"

"…"

$$$

It was a hoax. Above him, below him, on all four sides he could hear it. Telltale hearts of frantic keys clicking, creaking file cabinets, the whisper of paper. And, just outside his closed door, the rush of people working on something. He did not know what. He arranged his Money-Market™ bi-weeklies. He stared at the phone wondering why the receiver had become so heavy. He feigned interest in the communiqué e-mailed to him at an unreasonable rate. He kept the office door locked, incubated against the noise outside. The others' work became muffled and mumbled sounds and fury.

It reminded him of a story his father told him. He joined band in the sixth grade and decided to play the trombone. There was no romantic reason why; he chose it with little interest. He recalled the first day of practice. All were taught to take apart and clean their instruments. Taught about the reed and the valves. Taught to take pride in the authoritative gold gleam. The next practice they were shown how to make sounds by pursing your lips like this. But the third day is a mystery. Maybe the years wore through a day in memory, but his father insists he did not miss a day of school, and by extension did not miss a day of practice. Yet his friends and classmates on that third day seemed to know exactly where and when to blow, and how to read the music that seemed so enigmatic. Literally blowing him away. He could not read the music. He did not know how to move the slide into position to make the same sort of squawk as the others. It was as though he missed a day and they were ahead of him somehow.

There was the feeling Tom related to. Everyone knew something he didn't. Or learned it somehow and he missed that day. Smarter, better, taller, kinder, more honest, less perverted, wiser with money, handier with tools, more mechanically inclined, more organized, larger penises, more intuitive sexually, angrier, more focused, happier, gentler, better with friends, braver, more grounded, harder working, better dancers, less inhibited, happier, and on and on.

Still, around him, the other agents excavated the mountains of cold-calls. Each instructed to set a mirror on the desk and watch his/her face while they spoke to strangers on the phone. Smiling. A smile can translate over the phone. A voice with a smile will get better and quicker results. Better and quicker define efficiency. Tom's own mirror reflected only bewildered eyes. Behind them, Tom feared, was nothing at all. Sometimes, there would be a kick in him. An uplifting.

As if there was a part of him that would survive this, whatever it was at any given moment. A will to carry on and do something. He could tell that it was not innate. He had not been born with it. Yet most times, behind that feeling would come another nagging, darker feeling. Like a lightning storm behind the beautiful air it pushes through. As though that will to survive was born not out of Tom's genes, but out of some sort of catalytic event. A cataclysmic event. But be fucked if he could figure it out.

$$$

Kudos to the man (or woman perhaps) who invented call display. Kudos. And yet more kudos. It solved the mystery forever of who was on the other end of a ceaselessly ringing telephone. Before, all one could do was let the phone beckon and beckon. That nerve-shattering, trilling siren. Sounding urgent. Never pleading, always demanding: pick me up, now, dammit. Then the silence after. The ringing somehow louder in its absence. Who could it have been? What could they have wanted? What if it's an emergency? Then they could call back. What if they needed you and only you? Who could need me and only me? Your mother is dying. Your Uncle has been in an accident. There is an important, unscheduled meeting at work. You're late paying the rent. There is someone lurking outside your house this very minute, looking for a way inside, we saw them from across the street and we know you're home, too. Why won't you answer? The roof of your apartment is on fire. Your girlfriend has fainted at work;

she is in the hospital calling for you. They could all call back. The bad news would still be bad news.

How about good news then? Lottery? Promotions? Old girlfriend longing for forgiveness and lost days? Good news could wait as well. Good news travels fast, after all. Or was that the saying for bad news. No matter, the news would get to him eventually.

What could people possibly want? More disconcerting yet when the phone would cease ringing only to start up again. Demanding. He would dare pick it up and be trapped by the person he least wanted to speak with, whoever that may be. Telemarketer. Mom. Work. Even a possible wrong number could seem vaguely threatening and suspicious.

But call display? Misanthropic heaven:

250-865-1310. Mom. He would call her back.

780-356-8045. Uncle Rich. What humiliation did he need to bestow?

Unknown Caller. I don't know you.

Telus Mobility. Fine, I will pay it tomorrow. There was no need to talk.

He did not need to be accosted in his own home. It was enough he had to talk to people all day at work as part of his job. That was more than enough. So desperate had he been for a job that he never thought about the actual work involved. The recruiting process and questionnaires should have filtered him out. He should have been weeded out, as they say. He was not a people person. He hated people. Not in the aggregate sense, but in the individual sense. The screening tests he had done should have been 97% accurate to match his personality with the job in question. It was foolproof. Yet, the fool had fooled it.

He lied.

You enjoy working with others?: A.) Strongly Agree B.) Agree C.) Undecided. D.) Disagree. E.) Strongly disagree. He had strongly agreed. And he lied. *When you tell someone you will return his or her call, you do so in a timely and appropriate manner?* He lied. *You make decisions quickly?* Five minutes debating that one. And still, he lied. In the end, the tests proved him to be the perfect candidate for the insurance business. All based on his lies.

More lies when he reluctantly returned his mother's phone calls. "Things are going great, mom," he said.

"Are you working hard?" she asked.

"Not too hard," he said.

"What?" Her voice travelled up an octave.

"I mean, I am working hard, but not too hard to burn myself out." He corrected himself quickly. The lectures about work ethic from his mother and his Uncle had bored him since he was a child. He remembered his father and Uncle sitting at the table sipping beer. His Uncle was trying to get his father to work for him at the store. His father was saying he was happy where he was. His Uncle quoted salaries and prospects for retirement. His father smiled self-consciously and tolerating the ramblings of his brother-in-law. Tom's mother nodding in agreement as her husband struggled to hold his composure. "But I'm happy where I am." His father spread his arms wide in supplication.

"What the hell does happy have to do with it?" He remembered his mother or his Uncle saying.

And now, in that same tone of voice over the phone, his mother said, "Tom, this opportunity you have, you shouldn't waste it."

"Mom, I know."

"Your Uncle went to bat for you getting you that in with Walter. Now don't blow it like you've done everything else."

"Mom, what the hell?"

"I'm just saying, that's all," she was saying, "and please don't swear."

"Sorry," Tom said, reverting to a child. There was a long pause in the conversation.

"How is Edith?" his mother asked.

"Eddy? She's fine," he said and glanced around the room. Was Eddy even here? Then he saw her curled on the couch, half-hidden by a small throw pillow. Her hair thrown over her thin face, watching an aquatic documentary on the television with the sound down. "Mom says hello." He said to her. She waved one arm in the air, her bony fingers floating above her eyes. "Hello." She gurgled back.

"She says hello," Tom said to his mother.

"Is she working?" his mother asked.

"Yes, she's eating," Tom replied. Eddy looked over sharply and mouthed the words: what the hell?

"I said, is she working?"

"Oh, yes, she's working," Tom said. From her corner, Eddy shook her head. "What?" he asked her.

"Pardon?"

"I was talking to Eddy." Tom said, and then to Eddy: "you're not working?"

"Volunteering," Eddy mumbled, and then turned up the television a bit, signaling that her part of the conversation was through.

"You're volunteering at the pool? I thought it was a job job." Tom asked Eddy, but she was engrossed in the Jellyfish on the television. Tom could hear the narrator telling the audience about the dangers of these transparent creatures. Briefly, in Tom's mind, he imagined Eddy in the pool with one. Would they be able to spot each other in the water? Would the fish mistake her for an eel and avoid her?

"Tom?" his mother said, "Are you still there?"

"I guess so," Tom said. In his mind, however, he was calculating the rent and the groceries (which were minimal, but still) the cable television, the gas, the lights, the heat. With no income from Eddy, would his portion cover it? There was a draw on pay that he would have to make up. How many policies had he sold so far? Two? Both to himself. That would bring in some cash but maybe not enough. Could he sell more before the end of the month? Slowly he felt the hoax begin to unravel itself. The curtain pulled back to reveal the wizard as a short, overweight, balding, insecure man. The little boy stepping forward and crying out: "the emperor is naked, Ma!" The Grammy award stripped away from those singers, what was the name? Phony Baloney?

"So, work is going fine?" his mother asked.

"Work is going fantastic!" he lied. "I got a busy week ahead and some great prospects, so things should work out fine."

"Yes?"

"Sure," Tom said, trying to ignore Eddy glaring at him from her chair. He felt like throwing something at her at that moment but knew he would miss because the target was small. He spread his hands to her in petition and she shrugged and turned back to her jellyfish.

"I think this is it for me, mom," Tom continued. "It's a good opportunity."

"It is, Tommy," she said. "And we have the Lord to thank."

"I know, Mom."

"Have you and Eddy found a church, yet?"

"Umm…" He looked at Eddy, ready to look away should she roll her eyes, which she usually did when she overheard these conversations with his mother. "We went to this Catholic church the other Sunday, there."

"Catholic?"

He immediately knew his mistake, "No, no. Not Catholic, that's just the name, I am sure it was like a Baptist thing, or something."

"Why would they have Catholic in the title if it wasn't a catholic church?" His mother asked.

"I must have got the name wrong," he lied. "That's right, it was beside the Catholic church and that's why I got mixed up."

"All right," his mother said, "I've got nothing against the Catholics, you know."

"I know. That's right, it was beside the Catholic church. They share a parking lot. That's why I was confused."

"I doubt that," his mother said.

"Honest, mom," he said.

"No, I mean I doubt the Baptists and the Catholics share a parking lot."

"Oh."

"I've got nothing against Catholics."

"I know, mom."

"But I wouldn't go near them."

"You're right, mom."

"They have this belief about baptism that is just, well it's just all wrong," his mother went on. She discovered the Lord, or He had discovered her, shortly after Tom's father was dead. Reverently she grasped the church and the people as though she were the one being buried day after day, clutching to the pant legs to hoist her up out of the grave. Tom was introduced to happy, smiling, plastic people by the dozens. He and Eddy were invited to countless barbecues. Retching, Eddy always begged off. Tom was happy for his mother. His Uncle was disgusted. Yet, when he spoke to them both about their respective projects, his mother the church and his Uncle the store, it appeared they were speaking of the same thing. The sentences were interchangeable.

As in, for example, who said these words:

"The main thing is to get as many people through the doors on Sunday."

    a.) Uncle

    b.) Mom

    c.) Both A and B are correct

    d.) None of the above.

"People are attracted to a full parking lot. Attracting the people is what it's all about."

> a.) Uncle
>
> b.) Mom
>
> c.) Both A and B are correct
>
> d.) None of the above

"Once the people are inside they can (be) save(d)."

> a.) Uncle
>
> b.) Mom
>
> c.) Both A and B are correct. The parentheses around the word 'be' and the letter 'd' indicate that the utterances are so similar that they are in fact, the same.
>
> d.) Answer C is too convoluted to be correct.

So how did you score? Getting all the correct responses will make you look better. C? That's right, the correct response in each of the questions is C.

Tom wished he could find something that captured him in this way. Something to throw himself into. Something to believe in and give himself to, without reservation.

An aptitude test in high school had baffled his guidance counsellor. Students around him were impressed with their prospects of doctors, lawyers, and indeed, chiefs of large concerns.

Tom's results were inconclusive. He seemed to fit nowhere. "I've never seen this before." The counsellor said and urged Tom to take the test again. The results were the same.

"I don't know what to make of this," the counsellor frowned. The fluorescent lights reflected off his bald head. There were posters tacked carefully and strategically around the office, which had once been a janitor's closet. Each poster declared some positive message about education and children being the future of the world. A large map of the world served as a visual aid. Someone had written "you are here" in black ink with an arrow pointing to the North American continent. The counsellor looked at Tom as though his belief in these pronouncements about children as caretakers of the next generation scared the hell out of him. "Is there anything that interests you at all?"

Tom shrugged.

"Take the test again." The counsellor said. "And this time… lie."

When the test came back the third time, the doctored test, the counsellor proudly placed the results in front of Tom. Sales. This was what he was suited for.

Tom shrugged.

Tom imagined meeting the counsellor at a high school reunion, years in the future. The counsellor would fail to recognize the new, successful Tom. Tom would insist and procure a yearbook and flip to his picture. In his actual yearbook, which was tucked away in a closet, there was a dark shadow where his face should have been, even though Tom remembered dressing up for the occasion. The caption read: "Tom Ryder: photo not available."

"You inspired me to become a Life Insurance salesman." Tom would say at the high school reunion years in the future. But even in this fantasy, the scenario went badly. The counsellor held up both hands, "Don't blame me," He said and backed away. Tom's eyes followed him as the counsellor turned and searched out more successful progenies. There was one other of Tom's classmates who was in the insurance game in a different province. The man's suit bulged at its center and Tom did not get to speak with him at all that evening. Tom would get very drunk. Drunk until all conversations blurred and began to exclude him. Until he found himself leering at women's ankles. Until he threw up in the public toilet. Drunk until he couldn't tell or care who was in the washroom with him when he vomited. He found an exit without telling Eddy he was leaving and he felt better when he stepped outside into the cool air. He did not want to walk or stumble where Eddy or anyone else would find him, so he serpentined through the football field behind the school toward the black border that was the woods. He followed the trail for as long as he could until in his drunkenness he became disoriented and fell twice. He knew he lost the trail but still, he stumbled forward, knowing his direction would not lead to any specific path, but further knowing there was no actual path to be found. Until finally he broke into the open, found a convenience store and purchased an orange slushy. Even in his fantasies, Tom was never the hero of the story.

"But what God has given you now is an opportunity." His mother had changed gears as Tom's mind drifted away. "He wants everything for you. He wants you to be successful like your Uncle. Like that nice man Walter." Call me Wally. "You don't want to end up like your father working a small job in a small town making a small wage. God wants you to have everything."

"I know, Mom," Tom said.

"I don't think you do," his mother admonished. "I don't think you truly do know the gifts your heavenly father wants for you."

"I know because you tell me all the time," Tom said. Maybe too loudly. Certainly not loud enough to warrant the four-second pout.

"I'll stop now Tommy. But I wish you took it seriously."

"You are taking it seriously enough for the both of us."

"Tom," Her voice was stern, "you can't be saved by proxy."

There was another one. "You can('t) be saved by (P)roxy." If Proxy was a brand of some sort, like a laundry detergent. "Washed free of the past," was another. "Dad was happy doing what he was doing." Tom countered, or maybe simply thought it, for his mother went on and on.

"Your father never made a mark on anything. He didn't even seem to worry that you wet the bed until you were ten."

"Mom…"

"Well, he didn't. He didn't push you to do anything."

"He taught me to ride a bike," Tom said sullenly.

"…"

"I learned that from him," Tom said.

"Even that took a while," his mother sighed. "Listen, will you help me out with a church function next Saturday? A bake sale."

"The Lord bakes and the Lord baketh away," Tom said, and in the corner of his eye saw Eddy smile. Or wince.

"Tommy, don't talk like that. Tom, the Lord does not like to be joked about." She was speaking quickly now. Perhaps praying for him. But Tom was thinking about his first bike.

It was gold or rust coloured maybe. It was second hand, bought cheap or free. Much too big for Tom, his feet barely touched the ground and his arms reached uncomfortably and unsteady for the handlebars. Still, it was time he learned to ride. No easy task. Even learning to walk Tom held one end of a skipping rope and when his mother let go of her end he dropped to his bottom. His tricycle was not used to capacity, either. He preferred instead to grip the bars and propel it along with his right foot, his left foot on the backrest.

The bike too big or not, it was time Tom learned to ride a two-wheeler. His father steadied his hand lightly on Tom's back until his overstretched arms found balance. Then a push forward until they were both moving, Tom's terrified eyes watching the front wheel wobble while peripherally tracking his father. The drive was not paved. Small lakes were formed for Tom to splash in when it rained and then evaporated into deep craters he would need to navigate with the monstrous bike. His mother's car, too, would leave petrified grooves and rivulets, proving she was there that morning and promising she would return that night. At night Tom would lay with his father's shadowy form in bed and watch him trace Tommy's name in the dark with the end of a glowing cigarette.

Sometime during the inaugural lesson, his father removed his hand and Tom would ride until he noticed his father no longer supported him. Then the front wheel would shake anxiously as Tom looked behind where his father stood half poised to chase if it looked as though Tom would fall.

"It was stupid. So stupid." His mother would say years later. A bike too large, a road too rough, encouragement given in the form of chastisement. Tom would soothe her insecurities as a parent and in defence of his father. He did, after all, learn to ride finally. An empty lot down the street provided the smoothest surface to practice. The cracks in the pavement and the broken glass were too small to damage the tires.

This bike Tom kept for a long time. Traded, finally for a bigger one. Traded again for a motorcycle and again for his first car. Always in the car he would ignore the angry horns and finger gestures of others, leaving him wondering what he was doing wrong. Still he can feel his father's hand on his back the way an amputee can feel the pain in a leg that is no longer a part of him.

Chapter 5

It was probably in some sort of memo Tom never read, but who was this guy and what is he doing here? He was dressed better than many of the agents and fawned over by management. Sitting in the corner with a smug smile on his face. Smiling at everyone as they walk in as though to say, "you should know who I am." And some of them do. They are talking in an obscenely open and loud way for the occasion. The agents that don't seem to know who the man is file into the boardroom for what could be a solemn affair. Any speaking done is always in a low tone, not a whisper, but so low a tone that the intended recipient would be the only one to hear.

Finally, the man Tom usually saw getting out of a car in the CEO's parking stall stood and the room, to a man and as one man, swivelled their chairs to the front, rested an elbow on the table and leaned back. Tom followed quickly, but still was the last to swivel and lean, causing a few people to glance at him as though he'd spoken in a quiet movie theatre.

"Thank you for coming here today, I know you are all busy people," the CEO said, and Tom snorted. No one looked at him or responded with their own laughter and the mistake was tactfully ignored.

"The book in front of you," the CEO continued, "is one that's been floating around the office for a while. And I have given it to a few of my top agents."

A book lay near Tom's elbow. He had never seen it before. He picked it up and turned it over. There was a picture of the mysterious guest in their midst. The man was smiling out at Tom and looked twenty years younger. And bigger.

There was applause and Tom knew he had missed the introduction. The man on the back of the book, Travis Bunk, now stood before their boardroom looking humble and saying hello to the people he knew, despite having just spoken with them. This was the sort of guy he was, the back of the book told Tom.

"I thank you for that wonderful introduction, I am glad you liked the book and I thought we could talk a bit about it, first, and then be open to questions afterward," Travis Bunk said. "I wrote 'Choose Your Own Reality' because I noticed that there were a lot of sales-help books out there, and none of them really worked. So, I thought we needed one that does." There was mild affirmation from those seated around the boardroom table. "And I knew there needed to be an industry-specific sales-help book. Just for life insurance agents. Because I was one before I turned to writing full time. Wally and I are old buds, isn't that right?"

"That'$ right." Wally nodded as much as the folds of his chin would allow.

"Yes, we go back." Travis Bunk continued, "I was actually here at Consumer Life when I started out fourteen years ago. I worked here for two, oh, three months, I think." He shook his puzzled head at Wally, waiting for the man to take the cue.

"That $ounds about right," Wally said.

"Then I moved on to Ensurance, Ltd., I was there from '91 to '92, and then I was with Goto Health and Life from '92 to later '92. I worked as a consultant in '93 for a bit, but that fell through. We stumble, all of us. Let me be your inspiration. Umm, let's see. I sold for banks in the late '90s. So, I know the industry. I know it inside out. As do you."

Tom was convinced.

"Now, who can tell me about Capital Gains and why it should be insured?" He scanned the room and his squinted eyes fell on Tom. His hand reached out in what could have been meant as a welcoming gesture. He smiled and Tom could not tell if it was genuine. He understood fully what he had read about ironic smiles. It took nanoseconds for Tom to respond, yet in that brief time these thoughts went through his head: He is looking at me. He is gesturing to me. He expects me to answer, or smile back. No, no, the hand is out. He expects me to answer. What was the question? Capital Gains. Why insure against capital gains. It was pretty basic. He remembered the principles. But if he gave a textbook answer he would look like a novice in front of all the seasoned agents. And in front of the guest. He had to explain it in a certain way, in his own words, in layman's terms, that would make the guest and everyone in the room realize that Tom had internalized this information. He knew it deep, he knew it inside out. He did not have to simply regurgitate what he had read.

"The Capital Gains?" Tom said.

"Yes, why insure against Capital Gains?"

"Well," Tom cocked his head and tried to smile out of the corner of his mouth. As though this were the easiest question in the world. As though: where to begin, with words, to explain such a basic concept that should be tattooed on the minds of everyone. Like trying to describe how to ride a bike. Do you begin with something as simple as "Get on the bike?" If the question is this simple, where could one begin the explanation or answer? "Well…" Tom said again.

Quickly, as though it did not happen, the guest's eyes narrowed and his smile disappeared. The welcoming hand waved off to the side, dismissing Tom. Waving away a bad odour. Then the hand rose to the sky, leaving the question open to more competent men than the one Tom had been mistaken for. If this episode happened too quickly for the naked eye to catch, Tom felt it. It was internalized.

"Capital Gain$ Tax can put a lot of $train on an e$tate." Wally Russ began in a deep voice that was at once commanding and apologetic for having interrupted. His monologue was short and Tom recognized some of what he was saying. In fact, it was mostly taken from paragraphs three to seventeen on pages 96-105 of the training manual Tom read. Pure textbook. Yet the way Wally was saying it, the emphasis he put on certain words made the black dots Tom had seen on the pages dance around on a white canvas. Tom was beginning to believe every word.

When Wally finished there was an appreciative silence. The guest pulled a mock frown and nodded his head, deep in thought. "That's correct." Then the guest scanned the room again, wondering if anyone would counter such a reasonable and well-presented explanation of why life insurance is a good financial planning tool, and one particularly useful when planning an estate's Capital Gains at time of termination. No one offered anything.

"That's correct," The guest said, "and while it is absolutely, 100% correct," A long pause. An uncomfortable shifting in the seats. What the hell could be wrong with Wally's answer? The guest continued, "And while it's 100% correct, am I going to buy anything from you, Wally?" This hung in the air until the guest yanked it in, "And I don't mean to pick on Wally here, we are old friends." Relief laughter was louder than necessary, and Wally smiled, unaffected.

"Probably not on the fir$t vi$it." Wally spread his hands apologetically. Knowing what was coming, there was no need to argue.

"That's right! And why?" No one bothered to answer. Even Tom could sense the rhetorical nature of the question. Perhaps less rhetorical than narcissistic. It was a question that calls to be answered by the one questioning. "Because he told me a lot of crap…" This out of the corner of his mouth and his hand slightly raised in the caricature of informal confidentiality. The room is in on the joke. "He told me a lot of crap about securities and tax laws and all that mumbo-jumbo."

"It goe$ right over the pro$pect'$ head." Wally Russ spoke up. He would not be one of the ranks learning something new from this gentleman, he was in on the ruse the entire time.

"It goes right over the prospect's head." Travis Bunk held his hands out to Wally in congratulations. Tom could see others around the table nodding and he tried to make the light go on in his own eyes. His eyes, however, were not only unlit, they seemed to be transfixed by a knot in the grain of wood in front of them. Tom wiped the table with his palm as if that would smear the knot. He pulled his eyes away and toward the guest. The man knew somehow that Tom was the only one in the room who knew jack-shit about Capital Gains.

"They don't need a lot of mumbo-jumbo." Wally said to the room.

"They don't need it." The guest spoke louder, his eyes flicking to Wally in a veil of mild annoyance. This is my show. "But more than that. More than that." He was near a whisper now. "They don't feel it in here." Hand to his chest. Now whispering so Tom had to lean forward to hear. Travis Bunk softly beat his chest with each syllable when he repeated: "They-Don't-Feel-It-In-Here." Tom felt his fingers unconsciously tapping along with the rhythm.

"These people must be bothered enough, disturbed enough to make them want to buy. They must imagine a danger to their loved ones. They must put themselves in the position of worst-case-scenario. You tell the nice bedtime story to get the kids to sleep at night. You tell the real-life horror plausible nightmare to the parents after the kids are in bed. You pull back the curtain and show them the ugly reality that could happen anytime. Did you know one in two people will contract some form of cancer in their lifetime?" The guest stopped and pointed to Tom and the robust agent sitting next to him. "One of you will get cancer, it's a fact. Now, who wants to risk leaving their family destitute? Which one of you?" Neither spoke up. Tom thought of Eddy and found he didn't really give it much thought. Yet, he nodded alongside the man next to him. The premium from a new sale would mean money on the next cheque. Could he sell a policy to himself? What about Eddy?

"Not a good idea," The guest continued, "I have disturbed you, simple as that. A proven method for disturbing is outlined in my book. You will buy my product, not because of a bunch of statistics and percentages and mumbo-jumbo," he gestured to Wally who nearly came to a blush, "You will buy my product because you have been disturbed. How do you feel now, knowing that you could be leaving the person you are closest to totally destitute because of a poor decision on your part?"

He was looking and nodding at Tom. Tom's eyes moved back and forth, wondering if it was a question he should be answering. And if he did answer, would he know the correct response.

"I didn't think so." The guest leaned back, satisfied. As did everyone in the room, except Tom.

"$o give u$ an example of thi$ in the field," Wally challenged, to save face from his previous embarrassment in front of a lot of rookies.

"Certainly, Walter," The guest said, "Let's role-play a bit."

"Certainly," Wally said.

The guest speaker's face and demeanour changed, "Let me ask you this, Mr. Client," To Tom, it looked as though he were mimicking someone, or trying on a caricature of himself. Chin tucked in, eyes focused hard on the center of his glasses, chest stuck out as far as it could. "You have a spare tire, don't you?" He asked. Then his face changed again. His eyes bulged out and his lip hung slightly open, glistening wet that looked like drool. This was him playing the client's part in the back and forth "Well, well," He stuttered, "Waddya mean."

"A spare tire? In the back of your car?" He answered himself.

$$$

Tom left the meeting with two certainties. One: the guest speaker saw right through him and hated him. Two: Tom was going to have to read Travis Bunk's book. Disturbing people made sense. It was so logical and simple, yet the guest speaker made it sound as though no one used his simple method. True, Wally never picked up a copy when he left the boardroom, but Tom could imagine Wally seething with envy. After all, the guest speaker couldn't have weighed more than 85 kg.

It was also a certainty in his head, at that moment, that he would read the book and learn the method. He did a facsimile of a strut to his office and closed the door behind him. He turned off the overhead lights and switched on his small desk lamp for mood. He opened Bunk's book. When he was done reading the accolades from newspapers and other authors he never heard of, and the short preface in which the guest speaker told again, in writing, the spare tire scenario, Tom set the book down. He wrote in his day timer for the morning (which was fairly open) "Read chapter one of 'Choose Your Own Reality'."

The "y" in the last word grew an elongated tail because as Tom was writing the phone rang. He felt his chest flutter and his mouth go dry. He stared at the phone until it rang again. He reached for the receiver and untangled the cord and punched line 1. Dial tone. Had he hung up on the caller? No. Line two was for him. It rang. He punched Line 2 and cleared his throat into the receiver. "Tom Ryder speaking."

"Mr. Ryder?"

"Speaking," he waited too long to say, and said it at the exact time the caller said "hello?" "Yes, speaking," he repeated.

"Hello, Mr. Ryder, this is Rebecca from underwriting."

"Oh?" Tom could not hide his surprise. Underwriting usually just emailed him things. Not that he had anything to communicate with them. He had sold a total of two policies since starting, both on himself. He was working up the courage to ask his mother and Uncle Rich next.

"Hi. This is regarding policy #45933-002? We haven't received the oral swab from this client."

"Oh?"

"No. Did you send it in the package?"

"Well, I thought I did," Tom said. "but if you haven't got it then I must not have."

"Not necessarily," Rebecca said, her voice lost its previous edge. "There's lots of things that can happen to it along the way."

"Really? Like what?" Despite himself, Tom laughed and leaned back in his chair when he heard Rebecca laugh.

"I don't know." She said, "I'm new."

"Me too."

"Really?" Rebecca said, "A couple of newbies?"

"I guess."

"How are things going for you?" Her voice relaxed. There was a light giggle just underneath her words, as though any minute she was going to break out into laughter. Tom suddenly felt the same sensation rising in his throat.

"It's all right," he said, "I haven't sold much, yet."

"Don't worry, it will come. My husband did this for years."

"..."

"And it was slow for him in the beginning, too. But he did quite well."

"Is he still in the business?" Those words sounded awkward to him. The Business.

"No, he's dead." She said.

Tom sat up in his chair and felt his neck go cold. Stupid. Stupid. "Oh, I didn't realize…" How could he have realized? "I'm sorry."

"You're sorry? Why? Did you kill him?"

Tom could hear the background noise on Rebecca's end. No discernable words or conversations, just a babble of voices. Then, through the fog, he heard his name, plain as day, shouted out in her office, a thousand miles away: "Ryder!" He thought he heard his name called.

Rebecca's voice was close to his ear now: "Oh, shit, I'm sorry. Sometimes people don't get my jokes." Her smile came through the telephone. "It was ten years ago - we married young. He was a hotshot up and comer and he was killed in a car accident."

"That's terrible," Tom managed.

"Mm, hmm… it's water under the bridge, as they say. I'm past it; it was a long time ago. He's been gone for longer than I knew him." She paused. "I miss him still, though."

"I lost my father," Tom said before he could stop himself. Why was he telling this woman about his father? How had this conversation taken this sort of turn where they would be sharing personal information? A stranger. "A few years ago. It's not the same thing, I know…"

"No, no…" Rebecca interrupted. "In some ways it's more. I mean, your father, my God."

"It hurt," Tom said, "It still hurts. I'm not sure if I ever quite got over it, yet." There was the silence again. If Tom was waiting for his name to be called out like before, to be sure, it was only in his subconscious.

"His name was Tom," Rebecca whispered.

"Who?"

"My husband. His name was Tom. Like yours."

"No shit?"

$$$

Tom felt somehow compelled to take the sneaky back door on his way home from work. His feeble headlights barely found the road. Thankfully, the streetlights opened a patch of pavement and Tom could adjust according to the painted lines, watching the red flare of taillights in the vehicle just ahead. Drops of rain spat on his windshield and he grew tired of clearing it every few seconds, so he turned the wipers on low. More than necessary, perhaps, but it was darker just ahead, and it looked wetter as his internal compass guided him on a different way home.

Then there were trees. He remembered this. The SuperStore on the right. A graveyard a few blocks further up on the left. And it should be lit up with six of those overhanging lights. That one there. What the fuck? What is an i-scheduler? No, you idiot, you're looking at the backside of the billboard. As he passed the i-scheduler advertisement he looked in his rearview mirror as long as he dared without colliding into the cars next to him. It was well lit. He couldn't make out the writing but he watched just in time as the glasses dissolved. See? He looked ahead and peeked back only once or twice until the billboard became a blur of white against the dark sky. Until in his mirror, hanging in the middle of blackness, was the pulsing red glow of the city just below the horizon.

The mannequins flashed him and twisted their shoulders seductively when Tom pulled into his driveway. Tom avoided the nippleless breasts until a chill dripped down his spine and found a tingling pool above his ass. Get some fucking curtains. Now, and every time, the walk down the crumbling cement stairway to his home with the bulb burnt out seemed more frantic. The last leg. But anything could happen between here and inside. His foot sometimes overstepped the bottom step and it felt like finding, by accident, the deeper part in the water. Disorienting. Seemingly harmless, yet some have drowned.

Blindly, he dipped his hand into the mailbox and clutched at the envelopes inside, fishing them out and filleting the flyers right where he stood, by feel. His one hand held the mail and the other turned the knob and found it not giving. He alternated between searching his pocket for keys and ringing the doorbell until he heard Eddy's muffled voice from behind the door. "What? Holy shit."

"Hey. Let me in!" He shouted at the door.

"For… something… something… something…" Her voice was lost in the clicking of a lock and then her departure. He turned the knob and walked into complete darkness. In a few seconds, he could see candles of various sizes set around the apartment. In the corner Eddy sat cross-legged on the floor, shining a flashlight up at herself, her face glowing and floating in the center of Tom's vision.

"What the hell are you doing?" Tom asked the floating face.

"What do you mean?" Snap went the flashlight. Now only the three small scented candles lit the place. On an end table, Tom noticed four or five burned-out party sparklers. She saw him looking. "Well I had to get to the flashlight somehow, all the lights were off."

"And the other candles?"

"They were already lit," she said. "The furnace doesn't seem to be working."

Then Tom became aware of how cold it was in the apartment. His coat was still on, but he could feel the chill. There was no warmth hitting him in the face. There was no comfort here. He decided to leave the coat on. "The furnace?"

"I tried to turn it up and nothing happened. It didn't make a sound."

"It didn't kick in?" He asked.

"I guess not. It didn't make that sound when I usually turn up the heat, you know, that whhooomph sound."

"Hmmm…" Tom said. "I'll check the pilot light, I guess." He beckoned Eddy to follow him with her candle. They stepped slowly down the hall to the furnace closet. He glanced behind him to make sure she was doing all right, and her body seemed to float along in the darkness without a head. "Hold the candle up." He said. She complied, and her face looked hollowed out now, no body, but cavities for eyes and an elongated shadow of a nose, her mouth shaped in a frightening grimace. "A little lower." He told her.

Once inside the small closet, with Eddy holding the candle, Tom struggled with the faceplate of the furnace. It scraped and scratched until he was able to remove it and set it gently against the wall. He peered up into the darkness of the mechanism. He knew a little about the workings of the furnace. When he was small, maybe three or four or five, he would wake in his bed in the middle of the night, wondering about the darkness all around him. He would take his blanket and step out of his room into the silence. Always, he found his way to the furnace, which, in their old house had no separate room. It was in the middle of the living room, tucked away in a corner, inconspicuous to anyone who lived there and saw it often. He would make a bed for himself with the blanket and a pillow and stare up through the slats in the furnace's front panel. The small pilot light would burn steadily and blue. He would watch it flicker and feel his eyes flicker with its rhythm. Then, without warning, but as though he knew it was going to happen, the pilot light would ignite a row of yellow flame along its insides, right in front of his eyes. They would dance and illuminate the mechanical organs of the furnace until just as suddenly the row of flame disappeared and the lone blue flame was there again, comforting him until the next performance. He knew this much: you needed an initial flame to light the others, which in turn would make the heat necessary to warm the house.

"Do you have matches?" he asked.

"Just a second," Eddy said and swam away in the dark. He heard her stumbling around in the apartment while he lay there, his eyes involuntarily closing now and then, threatening to stay closed for a long time. Maybe they were closed for a long time. Maybe he slept.

"Here you go." Eddy appeared out of nowhere and his hands reached for the lighter. He flicked it and held it into the mechanics. His own meek yellow flame looked small and empty in the guts of the furnace. There was nothing happening. He found the knob and read the instructions.

1. Push and hold in knob

2. Light pilot light

3. Hold knob for three seconds after lighting

4. Release

Tom did as he was instructed and waited. Nothing. Darkness. Cold. He tried again. Nothing. There would be no reassuring blue light, there would be no dancing yellow soldiers standing all in a row. If the furnace was his amusement park as a child that would lull him to sleep, then this particular park seemed closed for the winter months.

The ferris wheel, the salt-n-pepper shaker standing still and useless without someone to start them up. All the popcorn and refreshment stands boarded. "I don't know." He admitted.

"Should I call someone?" Eddy asked.

"If the power is out, the phone will be out too," he said.

"I know," Eddy said. "I'll Google it. We can figure out how to start the furnace." Her voice was excited.

"Google it? On the computer?"

"Duh," Eddy said.

"No computer, Eddy. The power is out. Use your phone."

"But if the power is out we have no wi-fi," she whined.

Tom did not bother to consider the logic of this. "Well, what are you doing sitting here in the dark, anyway? Is it just our house?" He asked. He slid out of the furnace room and they made their way back down the hall. He followed the glow of Eddy's back. He fumbled his way through the kitchen and found a beer in the darkened fridge.

"Not like I had a choice," Eddy said from somewhere in the living room.

"What?"

"The lights won't go on. They went out about three and they won't go back on," she said.

"Did you check the breaker?" He asked and when she didn't answer he tried to make his way through the dim light to the bedroom, where the breaker box was located at the back of the closet. He reached for one of the candles on his way. Moving his clothes aside he held the flickering light to the switches. They were all in the on position.

"Is the power out?" he yelled from the bedroom.

"Um, I think so," Eddy shouted back, yet the irony was still apparent.

Tom gave her the finger when he came back to the living room. Her eyes were shrouds and he wasn't sure she noticed. "I mean, is everyone's power out?"

"No," She said and shone the flashlight at the ceiling. "Not the mannequins. They got lights. They got it made, up there."

Tom looked at the ceiling; the peripheral glow cast his elongated and jumpy shadow across the walls. "Then what the fuck?" He whispered.

"Maybe because we didn't pay the power bill," Eddy said.

"Why didn't we pay the power bill?" He asked innocently.

"Because we don't have any money, dipshit."

"Oh," Tom said. "I thought you were going to take care of all that."

"Tom?" She said in the dark. "Are you kidding? I'm volunteering. I'm frigging sick of giving my time to everyone else. Fuck."

"Well, should we phone somebody?"

"With what phone?" She was in the living room now. "They all work, on the power too, Tom. That's what you said. Should we check the news on TV Tom? Duh."

"Let's Google it."

"Fuck you, ok," she said.

"What do we do?"

"Use your cell phone and call the company and tell them how much we can pay," she said. "Then tell them to turn it back on."

"My cell phone?"

"Yes, Tom, your fucking cell phone. The number is on the bill. It's on the table. With all the other frigging bills." This last part lost in a mumble. She was moving slowly around in the kitchen. She opened the refrigerator door, as if she knew the light would not come on and she could attack the food unawares.

"All right, all right. Give me a minute to think."

"Are you kidding? I have been in the dark two hours waiting for you to get home with the phone." She was swaying in the dark, looking for him. He backed up as he instinctively felt her nearing.

"I'm just saying, if we're broke, then we have to watch our money." He pleaded, "suppose I sit on hold with the power company? I don't have a good phone plan."

"It's a 1-800 number, not long distance," she shouted. "Get the fucking power back on." He felt something swoosh by his head and he fumbled in his pockets for the phone. By its light he found the number and misdialed.

$$$

(Recorded conversation between Tom Ryder and Exclusive Power's automated customer service:)

Place: Tom and Eddy's apartment

Time: A few seconds later.

Setting: Very dark.

Automated Voice: (Extremely exuberant, but still automated.) Welcome to Exclusive Power's automated customer service. Please enter your 12-digit account number using your touch-tone keypad, followed by the number sign or pound key.

Tom: (Muffled, his mouth away from the phone) Eddy, do you know where the power bills are?

Eddy: (Unintelligible mumbling in the background)

Tom: They need our account number.

Automated voice: Or, say your last name followed by your date of birth.

Tom: (Away from the phone) Forget it. (Closer now) Tom Ryder. Sept. 6th, 1982.

Eddy: (Unintelligible mumbling in the background)

Tom: SHHH!

Automated Voice: I'm sorry (very recalcitrant) there is no listing for anyone with the last name Tomryder with that birth date. Please state your last name and your date of birth, and then press the pound key or the number sign."

Tom: (Realizing his mistake) Oh! Ryder.

Automated Voice: I'm sorry (very recalcitrant) there is no listing for anyone with the last name O'Ryder with that birth date. Please state your last name and birth date followed by the pound key or the number sign.

Tom: (Frustrated) Ryder! Sept. 6th, 1982!

Automated Voice: There is no need to shout, sir. Please hold and one of our representatives will be with you in a moment. This call may be recorded for quality assurance.

(There is maddening music too distant to hear. Worse, Tom can hear everything going on in some far away office. Nearly everything. Low rumbles that could sound like talking and laughter. Deep clunks that could have any origin. And underneath it all. Yes. There is the sound of a hundred voices in one room all talking quietly at once, and the smaller clicking of computer keyboards, a conversation in themselves…)

Belraj:GoodevenningsirthankyouforholdingmynameisBelrajhowmay Ihelpyou?

Tom: (somewhat startled) Hi, my name is Tom Ryder and…

Belraj: Do you have your account number, sir?

Tom: Yes, here, I think…(The sound of shuffling papers.) 167434689433.

Belraj: Thank you. (Clacking of computer keys) Just to verify your identity sir, what is your date of birth?

Tom: Umm…(Cough) Sept. 6, 1982.

Belraj: I'm sorry sir, I cannot verify that birth date.

Tom: (louder) What? How could I not know my own birth date?

Belraj: Sir, I cannot verify this account with your birth date. And you're not even female… (softly) ah, shit.

Tom: (Relieved) Eddy. Eddy set up the account. My girlfriend?

Belraj: Ok, whatever. I'm not supposed to do this. What can I help you with?

Tom; I haven't received a power bill and I thought maybe we had a credit. But now our power is out.

Belraj: It says the account is past due. Didn't you get anything in the mail?

Tom: No.

Belraj: We send the bills to… Hey! I think I know you! I went to this address in my cab! You were in my cab? The other day? You were the duck guy!

Tom: The cab driver? The actor guy? This is weird!

Belraj: It is weird. What can I do for you, my friend?

Tom: (Exasperated) I am going to kill my girlfriend! Upstairs. That's upstairs where they hang them. The mannequins. Our landlords store their spare mannequins in the upstairs apartment and some of the bills must have been going there. I swear I will take care of this right now, online, even.

(The remainder of the transcript is a back and forth with Belraj and Tom in which Belraj says: I don't know, and Tom says, Come on! And Belraj concedes and they exchange pleasantries and hang up)

Partial transcript of conversation between Tom Ryder and Christina Xing of the Ubiquitous Gas company:

Tom: (Laughing) I am not kidding you, I am going to kill my girlfriend. You know what she did?

Chapter 6

Twice daily his Uncle's staff cleaned the pneumatic doors of the SaveMart™ When the doors opened there was only the hint of the wheeze one heard when entering other stores. The doors were the quickest in the province. They never jammed. Patrons did not have to stamp on the entrance mat or wave their hands in front of the mounted sensor. The doors could anticipate your approach and slide open silently allowing entrance. If someone were to walk by too close the glass doors would rush open expectantly and then slowly close, embarrassed at having jumped to such a conclusion. Or bidding you to think again about coming into the store.

Tom walked in and said hello to the well-groomed greeter his Uncle always placed at the entrance. Always a fresh, clean shaved youth or a prim, sexless elderly woman. To his right, a bulletin board stated that no bills be posted without express permission from the management. There were no bills but that one. The cork was replaced on the first of every month to allow for a fresh-looking community board. On his left shopping carts glistened in the artificial light. There were no coin deposit boxes on the carts. There were boys to collect the carts in the lot; his Uncle felt no need to entice his customers to return carts on their own accord. Yet, despite this lack of motivation, the lot was always cleared and new gleaming carts awaited potential customers wherever they were, their placement strategically designed by Uncle for optimal pick-up and drops. Along the front of the store, the checkout lanes were equipped with clean, efficient women in matching uniforms, with their hair sculpted in similar bobs. Their movements synchronized so every scanner went off at the same time, so the random bleeping would be less obtrusive to customers. Box boys with neatly ironed green aprons scoured the aisles behind customers, replacing the things people took from the shelves and giving the store the appearance of being perpetually well-stocked.

One of the box-boys was removing groceries from a young mothers' cart and placing them in another despite her protests. Tom noticed the wheel of her cart was askew and spinning, not quite touching the ground. "It's no problem, ma'am, really," the lad said as he took her baby and an economy-sized package of toilet paper and planted them both carefully and expertly in the new, polished cart with all wheels making contact with the floor.

The cashiers smiled at Tom cordially. Although Tom frequented his Uncles' store infrequently, all staff knew him. Not that he was remarkable or especially memorable, but all staff had a collection of tapes to improve memory, required listening upon being hired. In this way, they could easily recall any and all items in the store, as well as names and faces of customers. His Uncle was so sold on the idea of the memory tapes that he had given Tom a set as a Christmas present some years before. Tom had tried the techniques for a while and then misplaced the tapes. He was too ashamed to tell his Uncle he forgot where they were and to ask for a replacement.

His Uncle's office was up one set of stairs and looked over the entire store via a one-way mirror. From there, his Uncle could watch all the aisles to make sure they were faced properly. As soon as a customer took something from a shelf, a box boy was behind them, replacing the item. The shelves always looked full and complete. Just as the floors always looked shined to a sheen. As well, Uncle had a direct view of the florescent lighting so that if one even threatened to flicker, its location was pinpointed, and a boy was sent up a precarious ladder to twist the bulbs or replace them. God help the boy who dropped either the new or the old bulb and let it shatter to the floor. It happened only once. The mess was cleaned expediently but the boy was not heard from again.

The blinking red lights on the security cameras guided Tom up the stairs to the office doors. He buzzed and waited. Soon the door opened and Tom stood looking at owl-like eyes staring through the crack in the door, darting back and forth.

"Yes?" Jude was Uncle's receptionist. Although she and Tom had met several times, Tom often felt that each time was a new experience for her. An unexpected visitor was a wrinkle in an otherwise productive, routine day. She did not veil annoyance. Tom thought of her as the moat guarding a castle.

"Hello, Jude," Tom said to the eyes in the crack of the door. "It's Tom Ryder. I'd like to see my Uncle."

"Do you have an appointment?"

"Yes, I do. We talked. The other day we made an appointment for today. Not an appointment, but we talked on the phone, and he said come by. Today. You know, not at any specific time, or anything. Or even necessarily today, even," Tom stuttered.

"So, you don't have an appointment."

"No." It was always an interrogation. She would drag the truth slowly out of him. "But I did say I'd drop by."

"…"

"Sometime this week."

"Might drop by?" The eyes bobbed up and down and the door opened wider, giving Tom momentary hope. But even he could not miss the irony in her polite screeching voice, "On the chance that he might be in?"

"That's right." Tom felt his scrotum tighten and a cool bead of sweat run from his neck down his back.

"It's a fairly unwise proposition, isn't it?" Jude opened the door wider still, "Taking a chance and coming all the way down here on the off chance that a busy man like your Uncle would be sitting here, waiting and wondering when you were going to show up."

"Well," Tom said when he felt she was through, "is he in?"

"He is in. Yes. But what if he weren't?"

"But he is."

"And if he wasn't?"

"Does it matter?" Tom spat, "I came down to see him and he's in. What could it possibly matter if I over-speculated? It paid off, I'm here, and he's here. End of story. Let me see him, the rest is none of your concern." He was sweating now. These conversations took place regularly enough for Tom to dread them. Always he felt the urge to throw something.

"Are you telling me how to run your Uncle's office?" Jude said after a moment. The door was open but she stood with her hand on the knob and her hip near the jam. "Because it sounds like you're telling me how to run your Uncle's office."

"I'm not trying to tell you how to run my Uncle's office," Tom said.

"Well, I'll tell you what, it most certainly sounds like you're…"

"Jude!" His Uncle's voice boomed from somewhere in the room. Tom watched as Jude's body tensed and her eyes went still and focused on something past his shoulder. As though she were listening for a faint voice. Or the next commandment from Zeus. "Do not badger the employees!"

"It's not an employee, it's your nephew," she screeched in Tom's face.

"Billy?" Uncle shouted, "What a surprise! Send him on in!"

"No, it's Tom."

There was a pause long enough for another droplet of sweat to make its quick descent down Tom's back. "Does he have an appointment?" his Uncle said.

Though his Uncle's office was twenty, maybe thirty feet from where Tom stood, he felt he could hear a sigh, the creak of a man getting slowly out of his chair and the trudge of footsteps to the door to greet him. His Uncle stood in the doorway and appeared the same as Tom always remembered him. He was tall, balding, and had large outdated eye-glasses that seemed to provide more prescription for his cheeks. He seemed to always look over Tom's head when they were speaking - or rather, when his Uncle spoke to Tom - giving the impression that, as with Jude, they were meeting for the first time. There was no familial greeting, no memories of the man when he was young. To Tom, his Uncle could have been any man he was acquainted with.

"Come in, Tom," his Uncle said. Jude disappeared to her desk and Tom followed his Uncle. It was like a parody of an executive office on the top floor of a metropolitan building. Instead of the windows facing a breathtaking skyline, his Uncle's view consisted of the tops of aisles of groceries. In his Uncle's skyline view, the sky itself was always overcast and gray and metallic. Mirrors placed strategically allowed a view between every aisle and Tom watched guests lazily placing items in their carts and box boys busily filling the gaps left behind. It seemed to Tom that his Uncle always had one eye halfway fixed on the mirrors so he could watch everything that went on his store. It could have just been a lazy eye.

Once they were seated properly with Uncle behind his desk and slightly higher than Tom, who slouched to enable the perception of power to tip further in Uncle's favour. "I know I called you and said drop by, but you should have made an appointment," he began.

"I was in the neighbourhood, though, and I thought, uh, why not?" Tom tried to remain relaxed and casual.

"Yes, Thomas, but other people have very different jobs from yours." He sounded like Tom's mother. He even took her mannerisms, as though they were brother and sister. "They are required to do things at certain times. Unscheduled interruptions are not a good thing."

"Can you actually schedule an interruption?" Tom asked innocently.

"Thomas, come on, let's get to the point," Uncle said. "But learn this valuable lesson if you want to succeed in business. Businessmen are busy people. Make an appointment."

"I will," Tom gulped.

"The thing is I had a little scare the other day, as your mother no doubt told you," Uncle said, reclining. "I was working late last Thursday night and there weren't many employees left in the store…"

…maybe just the janitors, who mostly wore headphones and listened to music. Uncle finished up with the ordering and scheduling for the week and let his lazy eye drift over the landscape of his store. And there, along the third spotless ballast, a florescent tube was flickering, and its counterpart was already blackened. He hesitated before making a note to have Gerald up to fix it first thing in the morning. He hesitated because he felt so invigorated after an evening of hard work, he felt powerful at that moment. He felt self-sufficient. It would take about a half-hour to change the bulbs himself. He wouldn't bother to call his wife; what was one more hour. It was work after all.

Uncle was feeling his age by the time he found the tubes in aisle 8 and pulled the extension ladder from storage. He balanced the tubes in his hand and climbed slowly, rung by rung, up the ladder to the ballast, higher than he expected. When he got to the top and realized he had both hands full and no way to change the bulbs, he cursed his incompetence and poor planning. In his haste, he lost his footing as soon as he began his descent. Sacrificing the new bulbs, he let them smash to the floor and threw his arms out to grab hold of something, anything. He was near the modest hardware section of his grocery store and as he fell sideways his belt loops caught on the industrial-sized hooks used to display the larger items.

He hung upside down perhaps six feet from the floor. He knew that were his belt loop to let go, he would smash face-first into the hard tile. It would hurt a lot and there would be bones broken and hospitals to attend. In that moment he knew he needed some sort of insurance. Not life insurance, of course. He could have died, certainly, but the thought was conveniently pushed to the back of his mind as his business concerns revealed themselves through his epiphany. What would happen, should he be unable to run the store? Would the whole enterprise fall apart? There must be some disability insurance he was lacking.

After one of the janitors arrived and got over a mild laughing fit and helped him down two hours later, Uncle resolved to call his nephew Tom. Yes, he would give his own blood the chance at a business venture. That is what family is for, to help with your business ventures.

"Tom, my agent is Wally, I don't think he'd mind if I shot some business your way," Uncle concluded. "So, do you have anything in mind?"

Tom didn't have a clue. "I have a couple ideas," he said. "I will put something together for you."

"Good." Uncle stood and by standing indicated the meeting closed. "Make an appointment with whatsername when you get something put together."

"I will, and thank you, Uncle," Tom grovelled while wondering about a commission on a policy for his Uncle. It would be at least enough to get the cable back on.

He watched Jude type. He thought she would acknowledge him when she moved to a new paragraph, or closed an application, indicating one job complete. When she did not seem to see him, Tom gently touched the side of her desk and said, "My Uncle wants me to make an appointment."

"What's it regarding?" she shot out at her computer screen.

"Insurance," Tom said quickly. "Life insurance. And disability, I guess."

"You're not Wally." Jude paused on her keyboard long enough for Tom to breathe.

"No, I'm not," Tom said. "I am helping Wally out because of my Uncle."

Jude clicked open her planner. "Thursday at 3:30. You get one hour at his discretion." She was typing Tom's name into the allotted time slot. "Please do not come early and stand around staring at me. And do not come late and put me behind." She peered over her glasses into Tom's eyes. He fumbled behind him for the door and skidded to the bottom of the stairs.

Tom floated on air as walked through the store. "Hello Charles," he called out to Charles. "Hello Carla," he shouted to Debbie who nodded and didn't bother to correct him. "How are the kids?" he said to a cashier he hoped had kids. He was elated. He had an appointment and, by extension, a guaranteed sale. A sale! It wasn't exactly what he was hoping for, it was a family member and not a true prospect, but it did fill him with a sort of confidence that had been lacking. He could do this. Uncle was frightened enough by his near-death (or near-broken-face) experience to think about looking at his financial coverage. He was disturbed. Tom saw the theory in action. You had to disturb the client. Tom was starting to understand. The pneumatic doors opened with a whoosh and in Tom's mind they rang out like a Ta-Da!

Chapter 7

Tom was lucky early in the week to draw a hot lead from a draw Consumer Life set up at a carnival. A clever agent lugged the water cooler from the office and put it in front of their booth with a sign that read: "WATER you doing without Life Insurance?" The cooler went glug, glug, glug as people were lured in by the play on words and a draw for a new television set graciously provided by pooling representatives of Consumer Life. Tom was not one of them; he was not able to pitch in to purchase a television. Yet, he was allowed his share of the names pulled from the draw box, complete with phone numbers and addresses. He promised to pay up as soon as his first big sale came through from the bounty.

All that week he pulled his list of names from the top drawer of his desk and sat with the phone in hand ready to call. He sat with a mirror placed upright on his desk and smiled into it for each call and each time tried to maintain his smile when someone hung up on him. Some were polite, some were not. Most merely disconnected without a word after 'hello' and hearing Tom begin his spiel.

"Hello, there, this is Tom Ryder from Consumer Life, we met at the…"

Click.

"This is Tom Ryder, we met at the business fair this past weekend."

"Who?"

"Tom Ryder, I'm with Consumer Life."

"Not interested." Click.

"This is…"

Click.

"This…"

"Go to hell!" Click.

Then, right when he was ready to throw in the towel, the one he used to wipe sweat from his brow every time he dialled a number, a man responded favourably. "Shit, I guess we should think about these things. We got twins, you know."

"Well, I know, and you really should," Tom stammered, excited to have a positive response after so many negative and hostile calls. "I can help you with this, it can be confusing at times."

"I'll have to talk it over with the wife, but you could come by, I suppose. Not gonna hurt a goddamn thing." The man slurred.

"Won't hurt a goddamn bit." Tom smiled into his mirror.

$$$

Tom decided to park half a block from his prospect's home so they would not look out their window at the sound of him approaching and see what sort of car he drove. "When you're dealing with people'$ money," he heard Wally's voice, "you have to look like you know what you're talking about." It would not serve him well if the prospect were to see him climbing out of his Cobalt. Suit and tie intact, but one hubcap missing and a dent in the rear fender, near the trunk. Where the spare tire should be. Did Tom have the spare tire? He made a mental note to check. Tom's mental notes were the equivalent of sticky notes of various colours that eventually get lost or thrown away. Thrown away usually because the message was outdated or the message too cryptic and the memory too vague to make any sense. And quickly this mental note was edited beyond recognition with this addendum: Try the spare tire routine right now on this fellow and his family.

As he approached the home he noticed the large pickup truck in the driveway. Lifted higher than usual somehow and exposing massive black tires. Surely getting a jack under that thing would be difficult. He thought of his own scissor jack in his trunk. Did he have the spare tire? The mental note was retrieved from the bin, un-crumpled and understood, for it was recent. Yet, the addendum was still there. Surely this fellow would worry about a spare tire for his family. Tom did a cursory once over of the vehicle. In the dark, he could make out a vague shape of wings or something painted white on the tinted back window. This framed by aesthetic chrome piping, curving and bending in a powerful, but artistic way.

Tom walked to the front of the truck. He imagined himself going up to the door, just like Wally told him, "Picture the interview in your mind fir$t." So, this was how he pictured it: Walk up to the door. He reached for the doorbell, lit with a soft yellow glow. The chime inside was pleasant and accompanied by sounds of cheering from children, obviously, and good-natured laughing from two adults. The door opened, and an attractive blond woman smiled up at him. She was bent over roughing the fur on a dog that sat obediently by her side. "We've been waiting for you," She said.

Tom smiled back as the woman stood. "Oh, good! My name is Tom Ryder I'm with Consumer Life Insurance." They shook hands, her small hands daintily pressing against his. And did they linger there just a little too long?

"I know, please come in. I'm Sarah." She pronounced it Sah-rah.

Tom took off his shoes at the entrance and put them in a line with the others ordered there, large to small. Sarah took his coat and hung it on an ornately curled coat rack next to a handsome leather overcoat. The living room was furnished with rich, dark cherry wood end tables and plush sofas and chairs. Strategically placed photographs adorned the walls. All black and white, all from various foreign places, all with an interesting slant to them, a picture taken by someone with a better eye than most. Sarah noticed him looking at the photos, "Those are mine," she said, "I took those."

"Wonderful," he said. Almost a whisper. He was entranced by the attitude and beauty the photos radiated.

"Thank you." Her face reddened and she smiled down at the polished hardwood floor.

Beyond the living room, Tom could see the dining room. Three people were sitting down to eat dinner. A man in a slightly loosened tie and twin boy and girl were saying grace. Sarah's place sat empty next to them. "Oh, my, I've interrupted your dinner," Tom said.

"Not at all." Sarah tilted her head so her hair fell over her shoulders. "We've set a place for you. This is my husband Joe and these two are…" Tom's fantasy did not allow for the children's names.

Through a delicious chicken dinner, they told him to feel free to tell them all they needed to know. The children ate and politely listened while Joe and Sarah asked thoughtful and intelligent questions throughout. Tom expounded on the necessity of life insurance, using examples and scenarios to attack the emotions of Joe and Sarah. He explained the benefits of Whole Life policies on both the children, the financial benefits the child would receive from said policies twenty years from now. And after dessert, the children cleared the table and Joe and Sarah glanced over the pamphlets Tom put before them.

"I am convinced," Joe said, nodding his head. "But you know, the tipping point for me was the spare tire story. That got me," he pounded his chest. "Right there."

"Me too." Sarah sat up in her chair. "I pictured it all in my mind and it scared me so bad I was ready to sign right then and there, it wouldn't matter what you said next."

"Definitely," Joe said. "Thank you for helping us out, Tom."

"It's nothing." Tom started putting his papers in his briefcase. "I mean, you knew the basics already. You insure your truck, don't you? Why wouldn't you insure the most important thing to you as well?"

Suddenly the truck roared and settled on a loud purr, jarring Tom out of his role-playing fantasy. Lights came on inside the cab, all manner of colours and blinking. The headlights, too, flashed once and dimmed, waiting for more instructions. Above the fierce-looking chrome grille, painted across the hood, Tom read the inscription: 'Nothing is more important than my truck.' Written in bone white paint with orange flames at the top of each letter. Out of his shock, Tom's mind raced quickly to the logical explanation; remote start.

Tom quickly tried to compose himself as he approached the front door of his prospect's house. $tay in control. Be in command of the conver$ation. Plan your talk $o it come$ off natural, but take the client where you need them to go. Now, ring the doorbell.

But there was no doorbell, at least one that worked. Tom jabbed the button but heard nothing from inside. He stood listening simultaneously to the roaring vehicle behind him and the non-existent noises from inside the house. Hesitantly he knocked on the door. As though the occupants were waiting for him, the door opened at the same time as he was knocking, making him reach as the door swung to complete his knocking. A woman in a large down-filled jacket slung her purse over her shoulder as she took a step forward, nearly bumping faces with Tom. "Oh!" she said in surprise. Her brow curled over her small close-set eyes. "Can I help you?"

"I'm Tom Ryder," he said, "from Consumer Life Insurance." He tried to smile but could tell by the woman's demeanour that she had no idea who he was. "We have an appointment tonight," he added hopefully.

"From what?" She made no effort to move aside to let him in and Tom shuffled his shoes on the concrete step.

"Consumer Life," he said. "We have an appointment. I spoke to your husband on the phone."

"Joe?" the woman shouted without taking her eyes off Tom. "There's a guy at the door here says you got an appointment." Tom heard Joe from somewhere in the house, his voice shouting something Tom could not decipher. The woman obviously could. "What is this for?" she asked.

"Life Insurance."

"Life Insurance." She yelled in Tom's face.

"Fuck!" Tom heard that. Joe's complaining voice grew louder as he walked through the house. "It's dinnertime," he shouted.

"He must have forgot," the woman said, sliding past Tom out the door. "He'll be down in a minute. I have to run." She offered no other explanation and marched down the driveway to the truck. She had to hoist her tremendous bulk into the lifted cab and Tom watched her back out and drive away, tail-lights occasionally flaming red.

Tom stood in the cluttered doorway. Coats, boots, school backpacks all lay haphazardly along the entrance. Tentatively, he closed the door behind him and waited. The living room just off the foyer was a mosaic of furniture style and colour. Spread across the laminate flooring were blankets, video game and DVD cases, some t-shirts and a large bone of some type. The bone was well chewed, and Tom could see the salt stains of drool on the floor.

"Sit the fuck down," Tom heard. "Hello? Sit down, dammit, eat! Hello?"

"Hello?" Tom said.

"Come in, we're in the kitchen. I forgot all about it. Sit down you two, what did I say?"

Tom picked his way carefully through the piles of laundry in the hallway toward the sound of the voices from the kitchen. Joe was ladling out macaroni dinner onto three plates. He had a handful of chopped hot dogs, which he dumped onto the plates and gave a casual stir with a fork. He placed the meal in front of two fidgeting children, twins obviously, from the matching unkempt blonde hair and the hard, blue eyes that concentrated on nothing but the leather briefcase Tom had gripped in his hand.

Tom entered the small kitchen and extended his hand to Joe. "I'm Tom," he said and smiled.

Joe looked at his hand for an instant and then wiped his own hands on his shirt. The grip crushed Tom's hand and he wanted to let go long before Joe chose to. "Sorry 'bout that," Joe said, "I forgot. You caught us at dinner."

Joe placed his setting of macaroni and wieners on the table and sat down. "Could we make this another time? Eat, for Christ's sake." The twins ignored their father's instructions and continued to slap and bat at each other. It appeared to Tom they were both trying to get his attention. The one on the left would splat her fist into the Kraft dinner, sending a yellow stream of juice up and over her hair

"Well… um…" Tom said.

"Fuck it, never mind. Let's just do it. What do you got?" Joe said and reached over to arbitrarily cuff one of the twins on the back of the head. Besides the misplaced hair, the twins had no reaction to their father's brand of discipline. "Eat!"

"Thank you for meeting with me," Tom managed, sounding small to his own ears. Remembering Wally's instructions: $peak with authority. You are doing them a favour, here. Protecting their family. "Let me ask you this, Joe, you have a spare tire, don't you?" Tom started.

"A spare tire?" Uncomprehending.

"A spare tire, in the trunk of your car?"

"I own a truck."

"OK, in the truck. You have a spare tire, don't you?" Tom gripped his case tighter. The leather felt sticky in his hands, he noticed his palms were beginning to sweat.

"Sure, I've got a spare tire, what's that got to do with anything. I thought this was insurance?" Joe blinked. "Are you selling tires, now?"

"No, but you have a spare tire, right? Have you ever seen it?"

"Of course, I've seen it. It's in the back of the truck, for Christ's sake."

"Have you ever had to use it?"

"What the fuck are you talking about?" Joe said, "Yeah, I've had to use it. Don't you have a spare tire?"

"No, I mean, do you have a spare tire?"

"I just fucking told you I did," Joe said and turned to his twins. They were looking at Tom the same way they had looked at their dinner. Half smiles and eyes that showed mischief, something that amused them. "Eat!" Joe shouted and turned back to Tom before he could see whether they followed his succinct instructions.

"Have you ever seen it," Tom asked. Where was he in this script? Had he already said that last part? Was he missing an important line that would lead Joe flawlessly down the path he wanted him to go?

"OK, look I've told you three times I've seen my goddamned spare tire. What is it with you and the spare tire? Do you need...? Oh, do you have a flat?" Joe's voice went soft. Tom had heard his Uncle use the same change in tone on him. When his Uncle suddenly realized that young Tommy was not being stupid because he was lazy or incompetent, he was being stupid because he was stupid. "Why didn't you say so there fella?" Joe said. "Do you need to fix a tire. It's those fucking kids; they play with my toolbox and leave shit all over the yard. You probably got a nail, I'm sorry. I told you kids not to leave nails and shit on the drive!"

"No, you don't understand, what I am trying to do…" *Is disturb you…* Tom went unfinished. And here is the fatal mistake of the man aiding and the man in need. If the weary traveller had placed his hands on the Good Samaritan who only wanted to aid, the scenario, or the perception of the scenario would have changed immediately from a man in need of help to a man attempting a mugging. Frustrated, Tom held Joe by his shoulder, wishing him to stop talking and get back on track. Instinctively, easily even, Joe shrugged Tom off and said, "Whoa?" his uni-brow somehow knitting even closer together.

Tom did not mean to grab the man. Tom felt he was not getting through properly. And when Joe turned to leave, apparently to turn the metaphorical spare tire into a physical reality, Tom couldn't help himself. It was as instinctive for him as it was for Joe to slug him a nanosecond later. Tom sprawled against the kitchen table, sending two-thirds of the allotted portions per child dancing and spilling across the table. At which the children, one out of alarm and one out of sympathy, lamented loudly.

It went no further. Both men realizing the enormity of what was happening, and what could happen. Things were calm except for the wailing children, prophetically sounding like sirens. "You better leave," Joe said, his chest moved up and down and his hand pointed in the vicinity of the kitchen's upper left cupboard.

Despite the misdirection, Tom backed toward the foyer door. "No, this is all wrong. You've got me all wrong, here." He tried to smile. In a parody of escort, Joe backed him toward the exit and Tom fumbled for his shoes, looking imploringly up at the man. "I'm here to talk about life insurance." His voice trembled.

"Huh?"

"For you and your wife," Tom said. "In case... and some life insurance for the children, too. Because I..."

"On my kids?" Joe exploded. "Cash in on my fucking kids if they die?" And said kids shouted even louder.

"Not like you think." This particular objection had come up in the training manuals. What was the response? His mind was racing, "Not like that. Money for their college, money for a wedding."

"Or a fucking coffin?"

But Tom was never good with irony. "Maybe, sure. I don't know how much they cost, but they're probably custom made and expensive..." Tom never got his ballpark quote out of his mouth. Joe's fist slammed into it so hard, it caused Tom to step back two steps, his head to relax and his tongue to taste blood. Enough so that Joe was able to shove him gently out the door and slam it in his face. The knocker knocked once, and Tom's body filled with rage. Which for a man of Tom's temperament consisted of:

1. Stepping back a few more paces

2. Staring at the door in slight disbelief

3. Whispering, as people will when punched in the mouth: "you motherfucker"

4. Then shouting: "You motherfucker!"

5. Retreating across the lawn as though ready to light out of the yard

6. Spying a stupid looking ceramic gnome that someone thought was a good lawn ornament

7. Angrily throwing this gnome toward the house

The gnome went through the picture window, parting the curtain like a strong wind and landed in the middle of the living room. The gnome shattered open, leaving white dust and dirt over the laminate. Joe appeared framed in the center of the window, his arms held open in the universal sign for 'What the fuck?'

"I am trying to protect your family!" Tom shouted into the shards of glass and the terrified children. He was heaving as he shakily made his way to his car. In his peripheral he could see/sense Joe leaving the living room and bounding across the entrance to the front door like a giant homing missile, intent on its target. Tom quickened his step and did not bother with his seatbelt. In his rearview mirror, it could have been Joe, a dark shape throwing shadows as it came under one, two, and a third streetlight. Tom stepped on the gas.

Tom thought all the way back to the office: "Failure Failure Failure." He did not control the conversation. He was unable to impart any passion into the spiel. Not only had he blown what should have been an easy sale - everyone at his office agreed that once you were inside the door, it was as good as sealed. Not only this, but throwing a ceramic gnome through someone's front window was probably not legal. Further, it must be against the ethics code he signed, some clause in that booklet. So, who would want to help him at the office try to secure a follow-up rescue appointment from Joe? Tom drove to the office thinking of quitting, of tearing the place apart, of shitting thin entrails of shit on those bastard's desks. Or of just sitting in his parking space and staring at the lit-up broken concrete wall until the auto lights went out. Call it karma, call it the plain old typical luck, but Tom could see before he got near the office that another car was parked in his stall. Or rather the place he preferred to park. He would drive home to Eddy instead. Come back to the office in the morning when everyone had time to digest the evening's events. This way everyone could be in the same room, and the morning reports they were obliged to give would be an opportunity for Tom to tell his side of things. At the morning meeting there was a chart on a whiteboard where Tom would fill in the week's activity like this:

Date:

# of Calls made:

# of Callbacks:

# of Appts Bkd:

# of Appts Sld:

When asked to explain briefly why the appts. Bkd. was not equal to appts. Sld. (rather, why didn't they sell every appointment?) most people could write or say the reason: Client had no money, or; very poor health issues, or; will call back. Etc. Tom would have to write: threw ceramic gnome through window. While that may cause more questions, it did put succinctly why the sale did not go through.

So instead of going to the office Tom took the next ramp all the way around and headed home. Which is where the other police were waiting. The police waiting at his office had parked in his stall at random. Because the RCMP are not stupid men and women it is ironic that some of their success relies on the stupidity of others. They parked a car at his house and another at Joe's residence, and at his office. Later Tom was to think how spooky it was that the police could track him down that quickly.

Unfortunately, the officers at Tom's underestimated his speed at arriving home. They parked their car strategically and one hopped across the boulevard to the Tim Horton's. Tom was able to get inside his house before the officer in the car realized the vehicle they were waiting for was already parked in the drive. For weeks the officer would be tormented at the RCMP Floor Hockey. He would blanch at the catcalls across the gymnasium, which were not far from the truth, like all caricature: "Ya, Louie, tell 'em I think I got the suspect's car." Others would shout back, almost like a call-and-answer rhyme: "You woulda' had the suspect if you kept your eyes off your hair." The officer in question was known for his vanity. He was rather good looking, yet needed always to reassure himself.

Even now as his partner crawled into the car with the mocha-whatever and a black coffee for him, the officer looked now and then in the side window. He began to see his reflection better. This was how he knew it was getting dark.

"It's getting dark," he said to his partner, "Let's see if anyone's home." They both got out of the car and walked toward Tom and Eddy's basement entrance. The mannequins swayed indifferently on ropes tied to the ceiling of the floor above.

Eddy answered the door.

"Is your father home young man?" the good-looking officer said.

"What?" Eddy glowered, and the policemen took an involuntary step back.

"I'm sorry," The good-looking officer said, regaining composure, "We are looking for Tom Ryder, my name is Const. Coxcomb with the RCMP, and this is Const. Thorpe."

"Yeah, I deduced it from your uniforms," Eddy sneered. She thought she heard Thorpe whisper: "Well, good for you, Nancy Drew."

"He just got home and he's in the shower." Eddy relaxed her hand on the doorframe and the police took this as a non-verbal signal to enter. She took their entering as a non-verbal signal that she should let them enter.

"We need to speak with him, would you please get him?"

Eddy backed all the way to the hall. "Sure." She frowned. "He's in the shower. Do you want to sit down?"

"No, thank you. We will wait."

Eddy stumbled down the hall to the bathroom. There was the sound of water running. She rapped three times and hissed: "Tommy!" She twisted the knob and found it open. She hurried inside and closed the door behind her. Tom was in the shower and she sat on the toilet seat, gagging a little. "Tom!"

"Holy shit! What!" He peaked from behind the shower curtain, his hair wet and dangling; he looked like a floating head. Lost from the mannequins upstairs, maybe. "You scared the shit out of me!"

"The police are here." She whispered above the sound of the running water.

He did not look as surprised as she thought he would. "Really?" he said, breathing a little heavier, "OK. No problem. I'm coming right out."

"What the hell is going on?" Eddy said.

"I'll be right out." Tom ushered her out the door and locked it behind her. He quickly dried himself and wrapped the towel around his waist. He stepped into the hall.

The good-looking officer was peering down toward him from the living room. "Mr. Ryder?" the officer said.

"Yes." Tom pointed over his shoulder to the master bedroom, "I was just going to get dressed, give me a minute."

"We need to speak with you Mr. Ryder."

"I can… let me be right back." Tom looked in the officer's eyes, trying to find some reason there, some fair play. He was in a towel, for the love of… He dripped down the hall to the kitchen where the officers stood, the bulk of their dark uniforms blocking most of the light from the table lamp in the living room. Tom turned on the overhead light. Eddy stood just behind Tom, glancing over his shoulder. The good-looking cop seemed to be the one in charge.

"I know what this is about," Tom said. "I will come with you if you let me get dressed."

"Know what what is all about, Tommy?" Eddy asked.

"We have had a complaint regarding you, sir," the good-looking officer said. He was twisting his head around, trying to look at everything in their small apartment at once. "No mirrors," he commented.

"I know there was a complaint about me. One of my clients called it in, I'm sure. Listen, can we just do what we have to do. Do I come with you, or…"

"What is this all about?" Eddy stepped out from around Tom and stood akimbo in front of the two men. "I do not like mirrors, if you have to know," she said.

"It's no problem, it's just funny, that's all," the good-looking officer said.

"I see my flaws," Eddy mumbled quickly.

"I know what you mean." The good-looking officer knitted his eyebrows together. Eyebrows that, every morning, grew new offshoots to be trimmed. A luscious lawn that grew thick and needed mowing every day, to maintain the overall effect of the garden. Always something in the mirror to make the cop feel unattractive, almost pudgy, shorter than other men. Even though he was pretty good looking.

There was a long pause between the officer and Eddy. Vanity meets vanity. A thousand compliments shattered by one imagined slight. It was a pause long enough for their emptiness to briefly inhabit one another's lonely soul, and then retreat, somehow more lost now from having known the kinship. The complete crippling fear of how others see you. Oh, the things to cover the flaws, the cracks in the dykes. Oh, the hair gels. The ex-lax.

"Excuse me?" Tom said. His hands were held out as though he were already handcuffed. "Should we go?"

The good-looking officer seemed visibly to shake himself free of a spell while his partner snorted and shook his head. "We just wanted to ask you a few questions and verify a few things, that's all, Mr. Ryder. No one is under arrest at this present time."

But could be soon, Tom thought. He could read straight through RCMP double-speak. "Can we sit down?" the good-looking officer asked.

The four of them stepped into the living room. Thorpe hovered by the television, thumbs looped through his holster belt. Eddy sat near Tom and the good-looking officer asked for phone numbers and other particulars, writing everything down in a small notebook. When he was through he looked up at Tom and sighed quietly, as though he was ready for Tom's story but had heard three or four that evening, so please don't dick around tonight. "Do you want to tell me what happened?"

"We had a misunderstanding," Tom said.

"Who had a misunderstanding?" Eddy asked, but was looking at the officer for the answer.

"Start from the beginning, Mr. Ryder."

Tom explained about the Life Insurance appointment and the sales method of disturbing the client. The misunderstanding regarding the spare tire analogy, the brief tussle. The gnome through the window.

"You threw a gnome through the front window?" Eddy shrieked, "what's a gnome?"

"One of those ceramic lawn ornaments," Tom said, shaping his hands into what he hoped was a facsimile of the gnome.

"Mr. Williams," the officer glanced down at his notepad, "claims you made very strong implications regarding the death of his children?"

"What?" Tom opened his eyes in surprise. "No. Oh my God. Of course not. Why would I… oh… wait, Ok, but here's how it went." Tom explained the benefits of insurance policies on children, the younger the better. He was speaking plainly, and the officer was nodding his head. Could it be he was merely acknowledging what Tom was saying, or was Tom convincing him of this topic? Why couldn't he have sounded like this in front of Joe Williams? Uninterrupted and relaxed he realized he knew a lot more about life insurance than he thought he did. After the plausibility of this was settled, Tom moved to more personal information. He does not know what came over him. He has no record with the RCMP for anything. He will pay for the window and the ceramic gnome and make an apology. He will give full-disclosure at work.

The good-looking officer wrote a little more in his book and then exhaled. "Well, Mr. Ryder, I don't believe you are a threat to these people. I am officially telling you now to cease all contact with Joe Williams, that includes e-mails or even messages through other people."

"Of course not." Tom bowed his head. Eddy was staring at him and he realized he would have to go through the whole story again for her, even though she was seated right next to him the whole time.

"Call us when that window is fixed; just leave a message," the good-looking officer said and handed Tom a business card. He then turned to Eddy and looked at her a beat too long. "And you take care of yourself, ok?" There was a real and gentle concern in his voice.

"Give me a break," Thorpe said, already out the door. The good-looking officer left. If he had tipped his hat at the lady it would have been a perfect exit.

Chapter 8

Tom could not leave his fingers alone as he sat in the manager's office at Consumer Life. He picked at the hangnails that his Uncle had warned him he would get one day if he did not care for his hands properly. His Uncle had taught him to push back and trim the cuticles, told him the exact length to cut the nails (1.6mm from the skin, in a neat arc with no discernable edges), showed him what the white clouds underneath the nail meant and how to rectify it, explained the importance of hand cream and the correct brands to buy. His Uncle's hands, indeed his entire person, was as meticulous as his grocery store. Tom, of course, did not keep up with the upkeep, neglecting its importance. Picking at the skin from his fingers in nervousness now, he regretted his remiss.

His leg began to bounce involuntarily and to stave off this nervous tick he crossed his legs. He noticed immediately one of his socks was inside out. Quickly he changed his posture, swinging his other leg up and over. This sock was all right but there was something white poking out from beneath the cuff of his pants. Tom surreptitiously smoothed his pant legs down with his left hand while plucking the mysterious object out with his right. It was a dryer sheet, somehow lost and lodged inside the pants after he washed his clothes. It survived three days in the closet, clinging despite the box's anti-cling claims to the inside of the pants, holding on until the precise moment when Tom could have done without it. It couldn't have fallen out on his way to work? No, no. Or in his own office while he was dabbing at his brow practicing what he would say to management when called on the carpet for misconduct? Right here, right now was the time it chose to appear and be dealt with. He felt the blood rise to his already reddened face. To cover, he brought the dryer sheet quickly to his nose, hoping the two men seated before him (or rather he before them) would mistake it for a tissue. He blew his nose into the sickly smell of pine trees. This caused him to sneeze three times in rapid succession into the fabric sheet. The fabric sheet now made good on its promise of no-cling, and Tom held the wet rectangle to his side so no one would notice.

"Tom, these complaints are not something we take lightly," the manager said gravely. His bulk filled the chair, his arms in his suit looking more like the arms of a plush recliner. The recruitment manager sat near him, just as large, closer to the edge of the desk. Tom shivered in an oversized chair far enough away from the desk so that he felt exposed. "It's not something we take lightly at all."

"That's right," the recruitment manager was smiling, "but at the same time, Tom it's not a big deal. No skin off your nose."

"No, that's not right," the manager said, "it is a big deal."

"No, I know," the recruitment manager countered, his smile faltering for the manager, but returning for Tom. "What I meant to say is, it's not something you have to worry about at all, Tom, no skin off your nose at all."

"Well," the manager cleared his throat, "It is something we as a company have to worry about." He scowled at the recruitment manager and the recruitment manager smiled and nodded.

Tom squirmed in his seat and held the snot-filled fabric sheet to his thigh. He nearly uncrossed and re-crossed his legs until he remembered the inside out sock that added to his humiliation.

"I have spoken to Joe Williams directly, both on the phone and in person," the manager said.

"A very agreeable fellow," the recruitment manager said and was ignored.

"I have never met with a man so angry, and I have certainly never had to deal with such a person so moved as to come down in person," the manager continued.

"The man really cares about the well-being of his family," the recruitment manager said, "and I think you did a bang-up job qualifying him. You get a guy that cares that much about his family and…"

The manager held one thick palm up to the recruitment manager's smiling face. "I am sure you have your side of things, Tom, and I would like to give you the opportunity to tell it to us now."

"The opportunity," the recruitment manager mouthed and winked at Tom.

Tom shifted in his seat uncomfortably. "Things got a little out of hand."

"Of course." The recruitment manager nodded sympathetically.

"There was a misunderstanding," Tom went on, "things got heated and…"

"You were assaulted," the recruitment manager offered.

"Sort of, yes," Tom said.

"What do you mean assaulted?" the manager pressed. "Did the man hit you?"

"It was very…" Tom found himself unable to remember the exact sequence of events. His mental continuity escaped him now. He remembered being angry, not scared, the way a victim of assault should feel. Or how he imagined a person would feel.

"So, you threw a rock through his window? His living room window?" The manager was squinting, his eyes lost in rolls of face fat.

"It wasn't a rock." Tom said quietly, "It was a gnome."

"I beg your pardon?"

"Oh, hell, a gnome? Phht…" The recruitment manager waved a hand in the air dismissively.

"A garden gnome." Tom held his hands up in what, to him now, was an exact replica of the ceramic garden gnome from Joe's yard, complete with red gnome-like toque. "Ceramic," he said.

The recruitment manager smiled and nodded, as if impressed. "Clearly self-defence," He said.

"Joe has agreed not to press criminal charges as long as his window is paid for and a formal apology is made," the manager said. "He wants us to fire you."

Tom dropped the snotty fabric softener.

"Here's the thing: Sam and I have spoken about this," the manager said, motioning toward the recruitment manager who looked at Tom and winked. "No one is beating down our door trying to get into this sort of career right now."

"We're lucky to have you." The recruitment manager smiled but the manager's face did not reflect this sentiment.

"We don't want you to see or even contact any new clients," the manager went on, "you can continue with any existing business you have or have in the works."

"All right," Tom said quietly. He was not fired? Tom thought he could count his existing business on one hand. Perhaps on one finger.

"There will be an internal investigation of course," the manager said, and the recruitment manager puckered his lips, closed his eyes and shook his head in a way that said: no skin off your nose.

"I appreciate it," Tom stammered.

"You may use your office and the facilities here and we would like to see you at the Monday morning meetings as usual. We'll keep this hush-hush. No one need know."

"No skin off your nose…"

"But please," the manager said, "no more rocks through windows."

"It was a gnome," the recruitment manager offered.

$$$

Tom had to walk past Wally's office on the way to his own and the big man called out to him. "Tom Ryder?" he said, rising with some difficulty from behind his desk and taking a few steps towards the door. Tom stopped and looked in. He and Wally had not had too much to say to each other. After all, Tom was new and Wally was a seasoned vet. What could the man want? "Do you have a few $econd$?" he asked. Tom assented and entered the room; Wally closed the door behind him and with one big, meaty hand, beckoned Tom to sit down. "I heard about your little gnome mi$hap," Wally said once he was assured Tom was reasonably comfortable. The chairs seemed to be made for Wally and men like him, Tom felt his toes barely reaching the floor and he had to sit forward. His nervousness had been spent at the meeting with the managers and he no longer even cared about his socks, forgetting even that he had left the fabric softener snot rag on the floor in the other office. "Do you need to talk about it, $on?"

"How did you hear about that?" Tom asked.

"I've been around a long time, Tommy. Nothing really get$ pa$t me in the office. If that water cooler out there could talk." Wally said and leaned back. His gut stuck out and his tie looked as though it were laying flat on a display table. He hooked two large, tree trunk arms behind his head and exhaled. Tom could smell onions and beer on his breath.

"I didn't really want anyone to know," Tom said, humbly.

"Then you $houlnd't have done it," Wally said, then burst out laughing. The room shook and the pictures rattled in their frames. "Ju$t $hitting you, Tommy."

Tom tried to smile.

"I wanted to tell you that, in thi$ indu$try, you will run into all $orts. You are not a$ unique a$ you think. I have had my $hare of bad appointment$."

"You?" Tom asked.

"Hell ye$," Wally said, and smiled. White blinding light filled Tom's vision. "I remember my third year I got into a fi$t fight with a potential, $ame as you."

"I don't believe it," Tom said, wondering what sort of man would challenge Walter (Call Me Wally) Russ to a fight.

"He wa$ a $ucce$$full bu$ine$$ man, thought he knew it all," Wally said, "Big a$ a hou$e. I $et him $traight. But I nearly lo$t my job over it."

"Wow."

"You bet," Wally said, "I want to tell you, though, you can't win them all. Thinking that you can will only fru$trate you right out of a career."

"I was almost fired," Tom said.

Wally roared laughter again; this time Tom did feel the floor shake a little. "Do you $ee how many empty office$ thi$ company ha$ right now?" Tom shrugged. "Too many. We haven't had a new recruit in a year or two. All the agent$ here are old hand$. A lot of old bull$ staggering around, clo$e to retirement. They need new blood and they will try and recruit ju$t about anything."

Somehow this did not make Tom feel any better, if that indeed was Wally's intention. He glanced around Wally's office. Paperweights held everything to the mahogany desk. Wally's screen saver showed a ball bouncing languidly around the black screen, bouncing off the virtual edges of the monitor. Fat families in heavy frames adorned the walls. When Wally leaned forward, his shirt strained against his chest and arms, making Tom think the buttons would pop off and fly right at him. Unconsciously, Tom averted his gaze in case one of the buttons would catch him the eye.

Wally narrowed his eyes. "How are thing$ going around here, Tom?" he asked. "You can be candid with me. I have heard it all and

I have $een it all. Hell," he chuckled, "I have probably done it all."
When Tom didn't answer right away, Wally said, "De$pite my gruff
appearance, I want to help. I $ee a lot of my$elf in you. I wa$ hungry
once, too." This Tom found especially hard to believe.

"Well," Tom began, and then felt it pouring out of him.
Perhaps it was the conflict with Joe Williams, perhaps it was the near
firing. Maybe it was the unpaid bills and the begging and humiliation
of asking for the power and heat to be restored. Maybe it was his fear
of being a failure, but he told Wally every fear, every insecurity he
had about the job.

When Tom was through, Wally let out a sigh and Tom looked
away from the onion and beer wind. "Do you buy the $tuff in the book
they gave u$? And the lecture?"

"The lecture? Disturbing?" Tom asked.

"That'$ right."

Tom thought for a moment. "The concept I understand. It
didn't work when I tried it on Joe, I failed. I don't think I got through
to him."

Another deep chuckle. "It'$ a good theory, and it doe$ work,"
Wally said. "The thing i$, you have to believe it your$elf. You have
to $ell your$elf fir$t before you can convince anyone el$e. Do you
have children?"

"No."

"Married?"

"I live with my girlfriend," Tom said.

"Fine, fine," Wally continued. "I remember the very fir$t time I delivered a death benefit cheque to a family. After that, I knew what I wa$ doing wa$ important. More important than any other job I could think of. $ecuring their future. After that, I knew there wa$ no way a pro$pect would get away from me. I knew what I had wa$ $omething they de$perately needed. That'$ why I am a$ $ucce$full a$ I am. No one get$ away from me."

"I don't think I can do this," Tom confessed.

"You can, $on," Wally said. "You can. All you need i$ a few $ales under your belt. Are you working on anything now?"

"Not really." Tom didn't want to mention Uncle who, he knew, was Wally's client.

"$ell your$elf a policy. $ell one to your girlfriend. Once the money $tarts rolling in, you get motivated. After that, the motivation will come from knowing you are helping people."

"I could sell a policy to Eddy, couldn't I?" Tom said.

"$o thi$ a$$hole write$ a book, give$ thi$ principle a fancy name and think$ he'$ being original," Wally said. "But we here at Con$umer Life have been doing that for year$. He call$ it di$turbing the client, that'$ fine; it'$ a good a name a$ any. All it mean$ i$ getting your potential client believing that he need$ what you've got to give him. And the only way to do that i$ to believe it your$elf."

Wally half rose in his seat, Tom thought. Perhaps he was trying to stand in the universal body language that said the meeting was over. Tom stood to save Wally the trouble; already a fine layer of sweat was gleaming on the man's forehead from the effort. Wally held his chest for a moment and then relaxed. "Damn." He said.

"Thank you for the talk, Mr. Russ," Tom said and extended his hand.

"Call me Wally," Wally said and gripped Tom's hand. Tom felt like he had stuffed his hand inside rising dough. "Go get 'em."

$$$

Once in his office, Tom could not face the paperwork he had to fill out. They wanted a detailed account of what happened at Joe's, and Tom found his heart racing and his rage mounting whenever he thought about it. It was all wrong. What was he thinking? Lucky he hadn't been fired. The recruitment manager had really gone to bat for him. But why? The only thing Tom could think of was the lack of new recruits. The manager talked to thirty people a day, he told Tom, and no one new was coming aboard. "We're taking any lame ass with a pulse," he said and Tom's face went red.

What he needed at that moment was to talk to Rebecca. He dialled the underwriter's number and extension, hoping he would not get a voicemail.

After three rings someone answered. "This is Rebecca Chimer." She said. Her voice was soft and he recognized it immediately. He felt the hair on his arms rise.

"Hi, Rebecca, this is agent Tom Ryder," he said slyly. He heard her tap at her keyboard.

"Hello, Mr. Ryder," she said.

"Tom."

"Excuse me?"

"You can call me Tom."

"Oh, that's right." Her voice went up an octave. It signalled a seamless move from business conversation to casual conversation. "My husband's name was Tom."

"I remember," he told her.

"So how have you been?"

"Professionally or personally?" he said.

She laughed. Three short spurts of pure music. A weightless bird fluttering above a rough sea. "How about both?"

"Professionally not that well," he said, "I lost a good sale last night."

"You can't get them all, Tom," she said quietly, reassuringly. Tom closed his eyes and nodded as though she were sitting at his desk and could see him. "What happened?" she asked.

"Ummm…"

"Sometimes people have no money. Or they need to re-evaluate on their own. Maybe the sale isn't lost after all, you'd be surprised," she went on.

"I don't think I'll be back to this particular… to this guy's place," he said.

"Oh?"

"We had a misunderstanding, and things got a little physical."

"You're kidding? What happened?"

"Well, he shoved me," Tom said, humiliated again with the re-telling.

"Oh my God!" she screeched, "What did you do?"

"It's kind of complicated," Tom said. "I threw a gnome through his living room window."

There was a long pause. "A what?" she said, her voice now sounded far away, her tone different, "A gnome?"

"Yes, one of those ceramic gnomes." With his free hand he shaped the gnome in the air in a pantomime he had done so often he could see the gnome just by moving his hands in a certain way.

"Like a lawn ornament thing?" Her voice had definitely changed, Tom thought. There was hesitation now and Tom could sense her frowning. "That's random."

"Like I said, it was a misunderstanding."

"The company didn't..." Hesitation again. Wariness. "I mean, you're still at the office? They didn't fire you?"

"No, not fired," he said. "Suspended, I suppose. No new contacts but I can still work on existing leads." Of which there were none, he failed to add.

"That is..." Pause. "I don't know what to say. You actually damaged property?"

"Yes." He tried to laugh at the absurdity of it all. All that came out was a rasp and a wheeze.

"Wow," she said. After a few seconds, Tom heard her clear her throat. The business tone was back. "Well, I am pretty busy here, I guess I should get back to work. What did you need this afternoon, Mr. Ryder?"

"Nothing really," he said, "Just sort of called to see how you were doing."

"Oh." Her voice was flat. She must be having a terrible day, Tom thought. It was perhaps a good thing he called. Maybe it would brighten up her day.

"We had such a good conversation the last time," he said, "I just wanted to drop a line and say hello."

"Okay..." she said slowly, "umm...well, listen, thanks for the call, Mr. Ryder."

"Tom."

"Sure," she said. "Listen, thanks for the call. I'll talk to you later. If you have any business that I can help you with, don't hesitate to call me."

"Well, I appreciate it," Tom said.

"Anytime," she said, and Tom heard the hesitation again, "You really threw a gnome through that guy's window?"

"I did."

"Wow," she whispered. "That's passion!" She giggled and Tom's heart flipped over.

After he hung up the phone, the conversation played over in his mind. The week had gone bad, but one phone call to Rebecca had made everything seem all right. Just letting it out to her about the gnome made him feel better. And what had she said before she hung up? Don't hesitate to call me anytime. It seemed she was the only one he could talk to who would really understand. A lighthouse in a sea of doubt. A buffet for the starving, or a sensible diet for the overweight. And now he was going to meet her. He had to meet her. Her voice was the exact image of how he thought of her. Her skin would be naturally tanned. Her highlighted hair would be pulled back, but not too tightly, enough to let you know that she could let it down, and when she did, she would be the most beautiful woman alive. And glasses, which she would need, but not wear all the time. It was like she was already familiar to him, yet, where had he seen her before?

The trouble with Joe and his job and Eddy seemed to dissipate. The sounds outside his office grew dimmer until all he could hear was the beat of his heart and a strange buzz, which he associated with the overhead lights and the billboard on the sneaky back door route.

Chapter 9

Tom heard it said, or read it, or saw it on television, that a person had no personality when they were alone. Meaning that it took other people to define someone. A person's character is only represented by the reactions to, or interactions with, another. In the same way, a question is posited about a tree falling in a forest. If no one were around to hear it fall, would there be a noise? A sound, after all, would have to be defined by someone hearing it. This always intrigued Tom, especially when others told him, when he was younger, that his personality was weak. That he had all the charm of a wet sponge, as one loquacious relative informed him. So, for Tom, not only did he have no personality when he was alone, it was apparent that he barely had one when he was with others. If Tom were a tree that fell in a forest he would not be heard even if the whole congregation of his mother's church were standing around and someone warned them with a well-voiced "Timber!"

"If you were a tree, you'd be a sapling," Eddy told him during one of their philosophical talks. He laughed despite the pang in his chest.

"If you were a tree you'd be a willow," He countered, but she got up from the couch and stormed off. Her feet barely echoing on the bathroom tiles as she slammed the door.

$$$

It took some convincing to get Eddy to accompany him to the bake sale at his mother's church. She barely spoke the whole way and only livened when they pulled into the church parking lot. The lot was full, but not only of church patrons; a small brewery shared the parking lot. Three or four older hippies built the brewery and made beer for the literary crowd in the city. The name of the beer was Art Official and the popular brand was their lite beer. Eddy knew one of the men that originally started the company and she mentioned this with a smile.

"Really?" Tom said, eager to have her talking again.

"Nice guy," she said. "He was a good guy."

Usually, the church had the parking lot to themselves, but today, in conjunction with the bake sale, the brewery was celebrating its 10th anniversary, so half the church lot was filled with Art Official Lite employees.

"Should we visit?" Tom asked.

"No," Eddy said, cheered already, "I don't know him that well. Let's see how your mother is."

Shocking, Tom thought, but encouraging. Perhaps the day would not be the downer he first thought it would. Eddy actually mentioned his mother's name without shuddering or throwing up. Throwing up, however, was not a fair indication of repulsion for his mother, Eddy threw up at the slightest provocation.

They parked the car and looked for Tom's mother. The crowd featured mostly white and blue hair with multicoloured blouses and purple pants slacks or checkered shorts that reminded Tom of the material he used to dry his dishes. Each woman commanded a post at a table with an obvious subordinate helper, also with blue or white hair and correctly uniformed. Plates of cake and cookies and other unidentifiable goodness crowded the tables and the modest throng moved from table to table, flattering the owners, sampling the wares and pulling exact change from their purses or wallets or waiting for exact change from the bake sellers. Eddy kept her eyes to the ground and let Tom hold her hand and lead her through the tables to the front of the church. Tom could see the minister by the glass doors, his white hair flopping in the breeze, making no attempt to smooth it down and smiling and chatting up an octogenarian. Tom waited behind the elderly woman.

"And I want to thank you so much again," the woman was saying. "I am so sorry I have to be off so early. Bingo at the home, you know."

"I am just grateful you made it, Mrs. Schmidtenheimer. Your cakes were lovely and raised a good bit of money for Somalia. I want to thank you, my dear woman."

"Thank me?" Mrs. Schmidtenheimer said, "For my cakes? Oh, thank the Lord instead."

"Well," the minister smiled, "they weren't *that* good."

Mrs. Schmidtenheimer seemed not to notice this slight, if it was a slight, and she left the minister smiling and clutching at her shawl. "Bingo," she muttered, and her hands shook a little and her eyes gleamed. How could she play Bingo with those shaking hands?

"You'd be surprised what these women will do for Bingo." The minister said to Tom and Eddy as if reading his mind. "You are Tim Ryder, am I right?"

"Tom," Tom said and extended his hand.

The minister shook Tom's hand warmly. "That's right, Rev. Tom Jones," he said.

"No," Tom tried to correct.

"Yes, Tom Jones." The minister tapped his own chest and smiled.

"Of course," Tom said, "but I'm Tom, too. As well. Tom Ryder."

"Oh, sure," the minister laughed lightly. "Forgive me, Tom. And this is Edith?"

"Eddy," Eddy mumbled to her shoes.

"Your mother is a very strong part of our congregation," Reverend Tom Jones turned back to Tom. "We are so grateful she joined our church."

"She speaks highly of you, too. As well, she speaks highly of you." *And all the time*, Tom failed to add.

"I'm glad," the Reverend Tom Jones said. "We are a family here and it's important that all our members feel this way."

"Have you seen my mother here today?" Tom asked. He felt Eddy leave his side and move to the edges of the crowd. Before he could call to her the Reverend had him by the arm and was leading him through the sea of blue and gray hair and polyester and pure white sneakers.

"I believe she's among the pastries," Reverend Tom Jones said.

Tom found his mother holding court with several other women and a scattering of bewildered-looking older men at a table displaying goods she baked. Tom had not known his mother to bake before, so he found it difficult to believe that the snacks before him were her product.

"I've found your only son, with whom you are well pleased, I'm sure," the reverend said as they approached. "Such a fine young man."

"Tommy!" his mother shrieked, and all faces turned to him. "You came. Now try some of this." Before he could protest, his mouth was filled with pastry. Soon women from other tables were introducing themselves and, instead of the customary handshake upon greeting, were forcing cakes and brownies and rice-krispie squares into his mouth. He smiled and chewed and tried to make casual conversation through mouthfuls.

His mother interrupted now and then with "this is so-and-so" and "this is so-and-so." And Tom nodded to each person and forgot his or her name immediately.

"So tell me," the pastor took Tom's arm and led him out of the circle of women while his mother winked at either Tom or the pastor. "When are you going to come to one of our services? Your mother speaks of you quite often and it would be great to see you in the congregation."

"Oh, well," Tom stumbled, "My job is… it's not your nine to five kind of thing. I work a lot of evenings and weekends, you know. You go to the people when it's convenient for them."

"Of course." The pastor led Tom to the edge of the parking lot away from the business of the bake sale. "I understand that sort of work. My brother sold cars for most of his life. Did fairly well."

They stood in the parking lot facing the Art Official brewery. Tom smiled and jabbed a thumb at the church neighbor. "It's too bad you have to share space with the brewery here," he said, "My mom says it's blasphemy." He hoped church lingo would ingratiate himself with the minister. He felt inexplicably nervous.

"She said that, did she?" The pastor glanced at his neighbour's building. Then his gaze met the swaying trees and the clouds above them. "Well, I'll tell you something, Tom," he said. "You mind if I call you Tom?"

"No, of course not."

"Then please, call me Tom." The pastor smiled. "I'll tell you something, Tom. You see that church?" He pointed back to the large building and the people selling cakes in the parking lot. Tom nodded. "That is just a building. And so is that." He lifted his arm to indicate the brewery.

"..."

"Many of these ladies here, and I'm not saying your mother, but many of these ladies here get offended by things that have nothing to do with the church. But you know, Jesus told us to live in the world, but don't be of the world, if you know what I mean. Or if you know what He means." The pastor laughed.

Tom smiled uneasily. "Actually, I don't think I do."

"Folks get hung up on things." The pastor was not smiling now. He was looking wistfully at his flock in the lot. "Legalistic, you know. The truth is if you believe in God and give your life to Him, then nothing else really matters. Was your father a religious man?"

"I'm not sure," Tom said, "He never talked about it a whole lot."

"The way your mother speaks of him he must have been a spiritual man"

"I don't know," Tom answered honestly and at that moment realized the pastor's hair resembled his father's a great deal. The same sweep of gray off the forehead, the same length of sideburns.

"Well, I would have liked to meet him." The pastor said.

"He was very good," Tom said simply.

"I can imagine." The pastor smiled. "Come to the service one Sunday, Tom. Take what you want, leave the rest. You don't have to buy into everything everyone tells you, but in my experience, it gives a person great comfort. Who could ask for anything else?" His hand was on Tom's shoulder and, rather than feel uncomfortable, Tom felt relaxed. It was like speaking with an old friend. "Just be good to yourself," the pastor said.

"Everyone!" someone shouted from the front doors of the church, "The Kool-Aid is ready!" The people in the lot began to gravitate to the church, mumbling their conversations to each other.

"Well, ladies," Pastor Tom Jones shouted back to the group, "Shall we?"

"Are you coming in, Thomas?" his mother called to him from across the lot.

"I suppose so, I do have a lot of things to do today," He said, "And I wonder where Eddy went."

Tom loitered in the parking lot watching for his dark-haired friend among all the white-haired ladies. Soon, he felt he was alone in the lot and he was sure he hadn't seen Eddy go in. "Eddy!" He called out and startled an elderly woman he did not see. She clutched at her heart and frowned at him severely and he apologized with a grim smile. "I can't find my girlfriend," he offered as an explanation, and the woman started on her walker to the church. He followed her briefly wondering if he should offer assistance. The scrape of the aluminum walker against the tiny rocks in the parking lot, the shuffling gait, it looked like an arduous procedure. But how would he help? Give her his arm? She had the walker already. Pick her up and carry her to the front door? Would it be piggyback, or would he just hoist her under his arm? Would he have to prop her somewhere while he retrieved the walker from the lot? What if someone ran over the walker while it was sitting there alone?

"Tom?" he heard. It came from far off. "Eddy?" he shouted again. He heard Eddy yell his name. He began to walk the perimeter of the church.

He finally found her between the side of the church and the near-empty back parking lot. She sat crossed-legged and gazed up at him with horror, her eyes wide, her face and neck covered with ooey-gooey goodness. Chocolate, whipped cream, marzipan… Her hands protected the bounty in her lap, stolen frantically from the bake sale tables.

"Oh my God, Eddy. Are you alright?"

"Tom… Tommy…" She gasped in ecstasy.

There was a scream as the woman with the walker found them and mistook the raspberry sauce for blood running down Eddy's chin and neck. The woman looked at Tom with a mixture of disgust and fear. She fumbled in her purse for either a cell phone or mace. Before she could decide, Tom bent and held Eddy's sticky hands to lift her easily to her feet.

"Get me out of here," Eddy screamed, with Tom alternately leading her away and keeping her hands from reaching up and shoving a finger down her own throat. "Please, Tom," she gagged. Tom carried her to the car.

She threw up twice in the car on the way home. "Eddy," he called to her through his own retching, "don't do that!"

"Oh my God," she choked, fingers down her throat. The chocolate had quickened down the front of her shirt. Tom stepped harder on the gas wishing to be home that instant. The Saturday drive to their apartment was different than his morning and evening weekday commutes. The traffic did not flow as well. Those driving during the week had a purpose and a place to go each way. Weekend drivers were impulsive in the way they changed lanes and where they decided to slow down or turn. Tom felt something near panic as he instinctively slalomed through vehicles, intuitively turning for the off-ramps that would take them to their neighborhood, their street.

The mannequins turned slowly to greet them as they came down the street. Tom shut off the headlights long before they reached the drive. Eddy pulled herself from her slump in the passenger seat and ran to the apartment door in quick, jerky movements. She didn't want to talk and she didn't want to be near him. She wanted to lie down in the darkness of their bedroom. Tom found he was all right with that idea as well. So he tucked her in and played her a relaxation CD of electronic cascading waterfalls. Though it skipped badly, like all their others, only this CD lost nothing through digital malfunctioning.

He retreated to the living room and stared at the telephone wondering if his mother would phone to rant tonight or leave it until Sunday. Maybe she hadn't been apprised yet. Word travels fast, of course, but perhaps she would have to gauge her response by the attitude of the friends bringing her the news. The Christian thing to do, Tom knew from their conversations, would be to pray for the person, not judge, and disallow gossip. So Tom knew they were all talking about it this very instant.

Tom knew people who would believe it to be their duty to let others know when they were going wrong. He knew people, and some former friends, who would seem to take pleasure in exposing another's failings in a feigned effort to help. Tom always thought of it as being nosey, or bossy. Or both. Tom was not like that. He would not point out mistakes, thinking instead that the person who perhaps needed correcting knew their problem already and was either a.) Living with it and relatively happy or b.) Unhappy as hell but unsure how to fix behaviour and/or situation. Either way, Tom was not qualified to solve personal problems. The best he could do had been written in hundreds of greeting cards already. In fact, the rare time he did try to placate someone or offer that person words of wisdom, the words were lifted wholesale from the type of feel-good junk e-mail one received daily. Yet, with Eddy, it was becoming increasingly difficult to keep his opinions, and even judgments to himself.

First of all, she probably wasn't healthy, either mentally or physically. Second, she was miserable, because she was undernourished and depressed about her body image. He wished he could try to be more understanding, but it was hard to live with someone who acted as though they hated you. He tried to be supportive; he hid the fashion magazines that always displayed the sickly-looking models she chose to emulate. He made dinner frequently and watched her pick at the food and later disappear into the washroom. Third, and he was ashamed to admit this even to himself, she looked like shit. Her bones stuck out in jagged edges everywhere he touched. Her face was sunken and withdrawn, her eyes dark, her mouth a grimace. She didn't look at all like the fashion models. Even they, with their protruding bones and withered faces had expensive clothes and lighting and professional photographers to make them appear sexy to someone. Yet Eddy looked like a toothpick draped in a sock. Clothes hung on her. Even her g-string drooped on her. The rare time she would let Tom touch her, he was afraid she would just break apart, like a treasure at the bottom of the sea, tampered with after hundreds of years and evaporating before the treasure hunter's eyes.

And fourth, did he really love her? He was not without his own problems, he knew. When they first met he was adjusting to anti-anxiety pills that made him feel weightless, or like he was slowly treading water all the time. She told him pills were nothing to be ashamed of and confessed her eating disorder. She ate too much, she said, and he complimented her on her figure for someone with that sort of hang up. She showed him her plethora of diet pills. Pills were just something to help keep the balance, she told him and he felt relieved. After all, the anxiety pills did level him out enough that, while he couldn't go back to college, he did decide to embark on the life insurance career. He was not much qualified for anything else.

When he decided he could not go back to school he tried selling cars. And this was how he lost that job: There was a client who he should have called on Thursday morning. Tom knew it was going to be a problem and he was looking forward to a long weekend and did want to be mired down with any customer complaints. Overwhelmed with his lack of productivity, he felt paralyzed and knew that getting away from it all for a day or two was the perfect thing. Monday morning, he placed the belated call only to discover that the customer's main and most fervent complaint was that he hadn't received the call on Thursday. The man was so angry that Tom defended his lack of action by telling the client that he was very sorry, he was away because his father died. The customer mumbled an apology and hung up. But the client immediately called again and asked for the manager, telling the manager that he admired Tom's work ethic so much, coming to the office so soon after his father passed. The manager then called Tom to the office and praised him for his work ethic and insisted he take more days off. Which Tom did. Only in the shower on some mornings would he question what he had done. When he got back to work there was a lot of sympathy and he had to force himself to mope around as if he really had lost his father. In a few months, he was able to pretend to be slowly getting over it. He carefully paced himself through the five stages of grief he researched on the internet. He circled dates on his small desk calendar with different coloured sharpies. The 23rd you will still be in denial, the 24th you can be angry for a few days. And he feigned anger, and people tolerated him. The acceptance stage was circled with green and he felt so pleased at arriving to this stage he was sad he couldn't share it with someone. But when his father truly died, for real this time and unexpectedly, Tom had to spend his grieving period going to work and smiling at everyone and anything. He found that the five stages of grief could not be scheduled and tended to overlap and return. There was Facebook, of course, so it didn't take long for management to say they had heard through the grapevine that his father died. Did Tom have two fathers? It was possible. But, no. Tom told them everything and was fired.

The balance Eddy told him about seemed absent in her life as they grew closer. If she actually attained her goal, whatever that may be, what would be left of her? What at first seemed to be a nagging inconsistency at the peripheral was now an all-constant center. Whatever the center was for her it blotted out everything else, including Tom. And Tom had not only grown accustomed to the back seat, he began to prefer it. He couldn't understand it so he left it gratefully alone.

"Why do you care so much?" he asked her on a rare moment he broached the subject. She was not in the mood.

"Your problem is you don't give a shit about anything," she hissed.

"That's not true," he insisted, while inside realizing that he had no haunts. There was nothing that drove him toward some end. There was nothing worrying him at inconvenient times. His inability to worry began to worry him. Then he would begin to feel offended. Maybe it is true, he thought, maybe I don't give a shit about anything. It isn't such a bad thing. In fact, it feels downright pleasant and relaxing. Who wouldn't prefer that feeling to driving yourself or someone like you toward some end? What would the end accomplish? And how would you know that you have reached the end you envisioned. "Who really gave a shit?" Tom always concluded.

$$$

"Eddy, this is going to sound strange," he said, "but I have a plan."

"A plan?" Eddy asked from her perch on the edge of the couch. "What are you talking about, a plan?"

"For our money problems," he said, and she looked over at him. He glanced away. "It might sound weird, though."

"What the hell is it Thomas," she said. "You're freaking me out."

"If we took a life insurance policy out on you it would mean a paycheck within say three weeks." He winced.

"Are you going to kill me?" she deadpanned.

"What, no, God no. What?"

"I'm kidding," she leveled. "I know what the fuck you mean. You get paid on a policy that you sell."

"That's right. That's right," Tom said, excited. The money would relieve some of the stress and pay off some urgent things, but the esteem was attractive. The esteem of taking something from payroll with his name on it. They would slide the cheque in the mailbox next to Wally's or someone. Theirs would be much larger, of course. Yet, it would mean he was in there. In the running. He felt his belt buckle inching into his stomach, little by little. Nearly painful. Nearly time to loosen the old belt. He hoped he conveyed all this to Eddy with his eyes, because he needed her to understand immediately.

"And what happens after that?" she said bluntly. "Maybe you don't sell another policy for who knows how long, and then on top of all these other bills, we have one more; i.e. my life insurance policy."

"But I will be on a roll." He said, but at the same time snickered at her use of i.e. which made his reasoning sound insincere. He wondered how he was to explain the concept of roll to her.

Her face suddenly contorted into a grimace that caught Tom off guard. She was crying. "I can't believe I am saying this, Tom." She hiccupped, "I don't believe in you."

"OK." He shrugged. "That's ok."

"No, it's not." She coughed each word out, "I don't think I love you."

"Ok." He said again. And shook his head good naturedly to reiterate.

"Oh my God!" she said. "That makes it worse. You aren't in love with me. What am I doing here?"

She began to flail on the couch, as if struggling to get up. Tom knew he should just be quiet. This could be another of her episodes. Times when it was dark out, with no moon, she would pace the apartment slowly. It was unsettling enough when it was raining and he would close his eyes at night and see her creeping around the living room, creeping over the furniture, or simply swaying like those mannequins right above their heads. Why didn't someone put up curtains? Could he demand that? To whom? The landlord would know. Perhaps the landlord and the owner of the mannequins were one and the same. Still, and better yet, why didn't they take them all away? Why only some? And then bring in more. It was so morbid. The way his headlights glared on them when he came home. He knew some of the figures so well he was saddened by their abrupt departure some evenings.

Eddy straightened in the couch, and calmly took Tom by his shoulders, looked in his eyes. "I will do this for you. But I am leaving you. I don't love you and I want something better for my life." She sniffed, and a tear/stream of snot went up her nose like water in a dry bed of a neglected houseplant or desert. "I will sign the document, but it's your bill, you show me where it says on there that you pay for it, because you and I are through, as of this minute. Done."

It felt so abrupt Tom's feelings were inclined to be hurt. Yet he felt relief. Two birds with one stone. There were times when he didn't want her around. He blamed it on stress. But there were times when he knew she didn't want him around. But who was to go, he wondered. Tom to his mother's? Not an option in Tom's mind. Did Eddy even have parents?

"I'll go to my mother's," she said. "I know you have a brother."

He didn't have a brother. Were they that out of touch? Did she have any siblings? He tried to conjure up a twig of her family tree through bits of conversation over the relatively long time they were together. She obviously knew nothing about him as well. "Well," he said with finality, "I will help you pack up your stuff."

"You can probably keep it or throw it away." She nodded at the floor quizzically. "I'll be staying with my mother." Tom wished he remembered who her mother was. He was sure he had never met her. The word 'mother' was suddenly ominous for Tom, and he felt an urgent curiosity. But it was too late. They were through. Neither of them were that sad, Tom thought. It was strange because they were both sad most of the time. Yet the word mother. It reminded him that he would have to phone his mother. For all he knew, Eddy hadn't meant the word ominously. Only Eddy would know how she meant the word mother to sound. And that would be left to Eddy.

"So where do we start?" she said.

"Start? To end things, you mean? Where do we start to end?"

"No," she shook her head sadly, already emotionally detached. "With the insurance you need. Where do we begin?"

"Right, that." Tom tried to stretch nonchalantly and reach for his briefcase. He did not want to tell her that he had already put all the papers in order and there were just a few things he needed from her. He pulled his case open and found the papers clipped together. He took his laptop out and plugged it in, smiling nervously at Eddy while he waited for it to boot. She sighed and looked away. He punched in his passwords and soon a calm blue screen prompted him to begin.

There was her full name, which he had to ask her to spell out. Date of birth, which he also had to ask, cringing as he did, but realizing by her quick answers she was not concerned that he did not remember when she was born. When the computer asked for her weight and Tom asked her for her weight the computer froze. "Full medical needed." The prompt read, and Tom cleared his throat.

"Eddy?" he asked tentatively.

"What."

"It says you need a medical to finish this application."

"Why?"

"I don't know." he lied. "Just procedure."

"Tom, you know I hate going to the doctor." She sat up in her chair.

Did he know this? "I'm sorry," he offered.

"For fuck sakes." She got up and headed to their bedroom, making Tom wonder for an instant where he was supposed to sleep. They had just broken up, hadn't they? Should he sleep in the same room? Should he automatically know he was relegated to the couch?

"I'll go first thing tomorrow. This weekend I'm gone," she said over her shoulder.

"That's great," Tom replied and sensed vaguely that it may have been the wrong thing to say.

Chapter 10

Why couldn't he, just once, jump into something with both feet and give 110%? He still found simple joy in what he always did. He still liked hockey. Not as much as some, who would paint their faces for games, but he watched for certain teams. He had a healthy appetite for sex, or masturbation at least. He hadn't lost interest in food, but was by no means overweight (he weighed 70 kg). He slept well and was not lazy, nor was he cutthroat. It was like he was an amalgamation of polar opposite parents. Or a middle sibling. He didn't have many friends, neither did Eddy. No real hobbies to speak of, so why couldn't he become one of those career men like Wally? Why couldn't he get interested in his work?

Still, there was this chapter in Travis Bunk's book that kept at him. More of a concept the man spoke about in the meeting. Disturbing your clients. They don't need facts and figures. They need to feel something. How could Tom do it when he didn't feel much of anything himself? He needed empathy. He needed to first try to put himself in the other person's shoes, and then scare the shit out of them. After all, he knew the fear and pain involved, his father was dead. Although he wouldn't use his own experience. That was too close to home. When he tried to conjure up the grief at hearing his father was dead, he knew another emotion was just underneath, as fresh as when it happened. The feeling was relief. And then shame at the relief. And then anger at it all again and again. Anger at his father for being weak in the eyes of his brother and wife. Then hatred and anger at them. His Uncle for constantly ridiculing his father, his mother for taking his

Uncle's side. Until time and time again, he could watch the happiness and patience dissipate and his father would glaze over and shrink from the hot air.

So, he would usher these feelings away. His Uncle was not a bastard. Not totally. He loved his brother, and Tom watched him grieve. Tom watched his mother grieve as well. Still, at the funeral, he couldn't help feeling he had watched them walk away with the look of relief. He projected on them his own taboo thought: "We are better off without him." But didn't that also include him? He could feel what his father must have felt sometimes. The time in the restaurant, where his father's steak came back three times and father still paid for it. Tom heard them arguing on the drive home. And then Tom's Uncle made a special trip over to the house that evening to tell his father off. "Those are spineless excuses, I don't know what you are talking about, what grand scheme of what things?" He listened to his Uncle raise his voice in the living room. And their reasoning began to make sense in his mind. Why did his father let that man take his money? And why was he listening to this from his brother?

And Tom had tried to sort out some kind of emotion that wouldn't cause him to run in the other direction. Bitterness and confusion, love and understanding. This one's too hot; this one's too cold. He thought a lot about his father, still. His mother didn't talk about him much and his Uncle rarely had anything kind to say. Although, shortly after the funeral, he watched his mother and his Uncle get drunk together. His Uncle, teary eyed, proclaimed, "He wasn't one of us at all. He was a saint. Like an angel." And his mother sobbing. Later, "He was so pure and better than all of us. We didn't deserve to have him at all." And Tom was confused again. There was no one to speak with about his conflicting emotions. He had no one to help him with the puzzle, to sort all the edges first, and then start filling in the middle. Anyone with this experience of loving/hating someone who is irrevocably gone could help him see things in a different way. Or more clearly. A new set of eyes. Or a pair of glasses.

Rebecca had lost her husband. The memory of their conversation seemed to jump at him from nowhere and so quickly he had no context for it. If anyone would understand, she would.

He was sure he had scribbled her home number down somewhere; she had given it to him, hadn't she? He finally found a 1-800 number on the back cover of a magazine and after dealing with an unfriendly operator who insisted on a credit card number (for identification purposes, Tom reasoned) he got her on the phone. "Rebecca?" He found himself out of breath, as though trying to find her number and call her had been a feat of tremendous endurance.

"Sure, it's Rebecca." The voice said, at first not sounding like the same woman at all. "Who is this?"

"Tom Ryder," he said, and clarified, "from work."

"Tom from work," she said, the sound of recognition in her voice. "And you are calling me at home. So, I take it this isn't business. Or is it?"

"Not business," he said, "Well, not really."

"Tell Rebecca all about it, sweetie," she said, and if Tom heard the ironic term of endearment, he didn't let on.

"I don't think I'm getting it. I just can't do it like Wally."

"Wally."

"Yes, Walter... Russ," Tom said. "You must talk to him sometimes?"

"Sure, Wally." Rebecca laughed. "Good old Wally."

"I think I'm failing." He felt the tension ease from his back the same time the confession left his lips. At last, someone to tell, someone who would listen without judging. Someone he wouldn't have to pretend in front of, who had no stake in his situation. To whom he had nothing to prove.

"Tell me all about it, sugar." The voice whispered to him, and so he did. He told her about Eddy, or lack thereof. He told her about his Uncle and his mother. He told her vignettes on his father, keeping them cryptic enough for her not to form an opinion on the man, one way or the other. He told her about his job, how he did not feel capable.

"Everyone hates their job, dimples," she interjected, "Do you think I enjoy talking to people all day about that sort of thing? It's mostly men and they can't think to talk about anything else. I get them what they want and then most of them don't even say goodbye, just, click... that's it."

"I like talking to you."

Long pause, "Well, you're different sugar. The point is, like it or not, I gotta' talk to them. It's my job and I get paid for it. I do whatever it takes to get that phone call over with. I know what they need and what they want. I do everything to get them that as quick as possible."

"Wow."

"That's right." Her voice, excited, still whispered and sent tingles through Tom's neck and back. She purred: "So what would, in your words, disturb those people into buying your stuff?"

"If they understood how easily it could happen, to have someone taken away from you so quickly," Tom said, "like you and I know."

"Yes." So near a whisper it could have been a thought.

"If they only knew that awful feeling."

"It could happen to anyone, at any time."

It could. And if it did…

"What?"

"I said," Tom said, "I knew you would help me see better."

Help me look better. See?

"No problem, honey." She laughed. "Are you sure there ain't nothing else I can do for you tonight? I mean, it's your money."

"Pardon?"

"I'll be Rebecca for you, honey…"

"I'm sorry?"

$$$

It was Rebecca that made it all so clear, he realized as he sat on the highway watching the billboard and the glasses fade in and out. She knew the business, and she seemed to like him. He could trust her to give him the real method. Not the textbook stuff they were trying to ram down his throat. The real secret. The key. Why hadn't he thought of it before? Kidnap Joe and prove to his family that the product Tom had was so valuable. When Joe is returned safe, what a different appointment that will be.

Could he really do something that some, that most would consider psychotic? Kidnapping? Essentially for ransom if anyone were to catch him and put two and two together. But sometimes two and two made twenty-two, as his Uncle used to say. Some plans could take something simple and make it exponentially better. And this he knew, or hoped he knew; Joe and his family needed life insurance. Simple. They didn't know it yet because they didn't think about these things every day. Who does? What person would contemplate their death every day, every minute? No one. So, it was Tom's job to not only make them aware that things like death happen every day, but more: they had to feel his passion if he had any. They had to be disturbed. It was obvious the spare tire analogy did not work for him, so he had to be creative. He had to create a situation that would blow the analogy out of the water. In fact, it was genius. Talk was just talk, he could talk until he was blue in the face, people just did not feel it in here. The reality of having her husband gone would become apparent if the man was actually gone. When Joe made his way home again, they would be clamoring for Tom's number. The gnome through the window would be forgiven; they would understand what he had been trying to do for them.

They would let him through the back door this time, as the neighbors or close friends or relatives would. There would be wine in the middle of the table and two glasses (she didn't drink), no need to rush into business right away. The twins asleep in their bed and Joe's cell phone turned off, they would listen to Joe's version of the kidnapping. Tears would well in three sets of eyes that evening, as the gratitude of just being alive welled and relieved their limited verbal expression.

As a capstone, Tom would present the documents to sign. Tom would be securing the safety of the man's family, and Joe would sign with one hand trembling, holding the other on Tom's shoulder. "I should have listened." He would say, through a mouthful of raven feathers.

"It's never too late." Tom would assure him, and present them with…

What?

He had to study. He had to put the proposal together. Whole life with a mixture of investments, modest risk. Tom searched for a pen and paper. He had to map it out, the different scenarios, the different plans available, which investments were attached to which plan. He had to have it down on paper so he could not overlook any detail. It would be a perfect deal. First, he would break in through the back door. If there was a dog, Tom would feed it some sort meat or something with pills in it. Could you drug a dog that quickly? How long does it actually take? He would have to test something. Not Eddy. Where would he plant the pills, in food? He would have to perform the experiment on himself.

Tom took four or five sleeping pills (one dropped on the floor and Tom thought he found it, but it tasted like what could have been a smartie with the colour sucked off.) Then he drank three cups of Neo Citron. He balanced a saucer, ever so precariously, on the rubber buttons of a stopwatch resting on the table in front of him. When his head hit the saucer, the stopwatch would let him know how long it had taken. If he needed it to work sooner and longer, he would double the dosages. Except, wait. There was something about exponential power. He should triple it.

In less than ten minutes after the dosage, Tom's mind wandered, and his tongue felt thick and hairy. The room alternated between bright illumination and dark and sinister shadows. He held his face in his hands and felt as though he were suffocating.

His forehead broke the plate and a tiny shard clung to his skin as he lifted his head. "Oww!" He said, fingering the gash in his head.

"Shit." He diagnosed further. Tom couldn't read the stopwatch, the way it blurred in and out and loomed large in his memory, although he was looking right at it. He slumped to the floor trying to clean the broken plate. The cool of the linoleum left him there for what could have been hours. He did manage to weave down the hall to the bathroom. It was shock from there, mostly, that kept him awake long enough to remove the shard of plate from his head and put what he thought was a maxi-pad on the cut. This is how he woke up, sixteen hours later with a headache made exponentially worse because of either hangover or wounded head. There was a tampon taped to his forehead and a stopwatch that read 16:41:30…31…32… It had not stopped when it should have, rendering Tom's experiment ruined. Except Tom had conceived the plan so quickly, executed it when he was under sedation, and slept so soundly he could not remember ever having made any such experiments and as such was at a loss to explain the cuts or the stopwatch.

Later, when he pieced the afternoon together he concluded that Joe Williams didn't have a dog, anyway. They didn't the last time he was there. Or did they? Forget the dog.

The plan needn't be so complicated. Kids are always making a lot of noise. And that large woman, the one that reminded Tom of someone's Uncle, would be at weight-watchers Thursday. Or was it Tuesday. Just walk up to the back door and knock loudly. He comes to the door, and Tom would say, I need a spare tire. And then… wham… no, that won't work. How would you get that big fellow out the back door? And how hard did you really have to hit someone to knock them out for a long time? Tom had never seen anyone dragged around unconscious like they do on TV. Tom had trouble killing a mouse when the need arose. He and Eddy found a mouse half alive in a trap they set, and it fell to Tom to kill the creature. He took it out to the front steps with a hammer and tried to bash its head in with his own eyes closed. He missed and felt the ricochet on the cement shock his forearm and shoulder. He finally managed to kill it after several bashes, but by then the mouse had given up its struggle, no doubt hoping Tom's aim would improve and end its suffering, and Tom cried a little. Cried for the mess on the steps, which Eddy had to clean, and for his own humanity. Could he actually hit another human being with a… what? Tire iron probably. It made sense. Hard enough? Would he squirm and blanch off last minute, causing necessity to strike not once, but two or even four times.

Fuck that, he decided. The man had to be coerced out of his house. Into his own truck. No, Tom's vehicle parked a block away. The noise the truck made would surely cause Tom to lose his nerve. He nearly pissed his pants when it started up the time he was there for the appointment. Once in Tom's vehicle, the trunk would be the best bet, Tom could drive the man to some locale away from town. Far enough away that the man would have to walk for hours perhaps, but not far enough away to make it dangerous. The man had to know where he was to make it home. Should he do up a ransom note to make it even more frightening? What would he say? How much would they be willing to part with? Not that Tom would ever take any ransom. The point was to disturb the family enough so that the next time they met with Tom they would be far more receptive to the idea of life insurance. After all, hadn't the note said that Joe would be killed if they did not come up with X amount of dollars? Wouldn't that bring his mortality close to home? Once he was reunited with his wife and children, wouldn't they realize how close they came to losing him, and wouldn't they focus more on their finances if he had been killed. Wouldn't they see that it could happen anytime, to anyone?

The ends justified the means. It was a terrible thing Tom was contemplating, he knew, but if the family were disturbed enough to want to protect themselves, then Tom had done his job. More than that, he went beyond the call of duty to perform his duties and inform the client. If it went as planned Tom would want to tell Wally what he had done. But he knew he couldn't. If only he could tell someone. Rebecca, sure, but someone in the office. Let them know he wasn't a lightweight. He would swoop in like a guardian angel and save the family from future and certain financial devastation. He would be invited, the next time around, to macaroni and cheese with the children.

Next, Tom tried to disguise his voice and practiced a menacing glare in the mirror, though he knew he could never let Joe see his face. He tried the Darth Vader voice, but it sounded too much like Darth Vader. He tried Clint Eastwood and that seemed menacing enough. He tried an evil laugh that ended up sounding like a demented Peewee Herman giggle so he scrapped this idea.

The main problem would be how to get Joe out of his house and into Tom's car. Tom did not have a gun, did not even know where to get a gun. Besides, he did not want to use a gun. He did not want to hurt the man. With a gun anything could go wrong. The point was to disturb, not destroy.

Then, later, he drove out to the billboard and began to make his notes. Under that beautiful watchful eye blinking languidly, he and Rebecca's plan formulated and took on a life its own. Now, it became no longer a means to Tom's end, but the very end itself. The kidnapping had to go so smoothly; Tom could not afford the luxury of celebrating the perfect sale. The endeavor would create so much goodwill with the victim. They would be grateful, downright fucking grateful to sign a paper that guaranteed them financial security for their family. Now that they knew how easily it could happen, at any moment. At. Any. Moment. Tom was already practicing the sales pitch once the client was found and returned safely to his home. He rehearsed moving his face around in the side mirrors of the car. He imagined not only the fat commission on the sale, but the adoration of the people in his office. Respect. He wondered if maybe he wasn't gaining weight and shifted uncomfortably against the seatbelt.

When he had scratched ideas down and brainstormed until he was having trouble with his vision, he hid the folded sheets of paper between the cover of the seat in the passenger side. He couldn't help smiling a little as he reclined back and pushed the steering wheel as far as it would go away from him. His eyes adjusted, and he gazed at the billboard. The glasses faded in and out three times as he let his mind wander. We help you look better. See? Yes, he did see. Rebecca had cleared it all up for him. The glasses came off. You get a different chick. See?

He was gaining weight. He could feel his stomach straining against the restraint. He shifted comfortably and traced his thumb along the polyester until he found the latch. Just a tiny pressure there and, snip, the belt slurped away. Tom opened his pants to adjust his underwear. Seriously, a little paunch happening there. He pulled up his shirt and moved around until his pants were out of the way. There did seem to be a slight camber in the hairline from his belly button to his pubic hair. He would have to straighten out more to be sure. If the pants were off he would be able to stretch right out in the car, enough to see if he was getting a little pot-bellied. He wiggled his pants and underwear to his knees. He levered the steering wheel as far up as it could go and hoisted his hips to the ceiling.

His plans were suddenly interrupted by flashing in his rearview mirror, lighting up the car interior with red and blue lights, waning and waxing frantically. Aware of his surroundings once more, he tried to stuff himself back into his pants. There were three sharp knocks on his window and then a flashlight beam directly in his face when he turned his head. A muffled voice said something about rolling down the window or getting out of the car. Given the circumstances Tom suspected it was one of the two. And while he preferred the former, the officer was already opening his door.

Tom recognized the officer who stepped back to let him climb out of the car. He pulled up his pants just as the officer recognized him. It was Constable Thorpe. "Holy shit," he said, and turning to his squad car waved to the driver. "It's Tom Ryder and he's jerking off in public."

"Allegedly," came a muffled reply, but the good-looking officer stepped out and came over slowly. "What are we up to tonight, Mr. Ryder?"

"It's not what it looks like," Tom stammered and could not find the hole in his belt loop. "I was just feeling my body."

"Ha!" Thorpe shouted.

"No, I mean, my gut. I think I'm getting fat!" Tom said as if he were proud.

The good-looking cop shined his flashlight so Tom could get his belt on properly and then said, "Mr. Ryder look, I think you're a decent fellow, and your girlfriend is very nice." He cleared his throat. "I don't want to have to be a part of an embarrassing situation."

"I don't either," Tom reassured him.

"No of course not." The good-looking officer went on, "I want you to do me a favour, ok?"

"Me?"

"I want you to go down to a mental health clinic, the one on Queensway. I want you to talk to someone there. If I let you go tonight, will you do that for me?"

"Yes, sure. I mean, yes. Yes," Tom said, "I will."

"I am going to check up on that, Mr. Ryder," the good-looking officer said, already retreating to his car. He was smiling broadly, "We have a deal now."

"We do." Tom waved and smiled as cheerfully as he could. As the squad car pulled away the siren let out a quick, deep 'whoop' that sounded eerily like laughter from inside the car.

156

Chapter 11

Tom's only experience with psychologists was from TV. He was strangely unnerved to find himself in a doctor's office that resembled any other doctor's office he had ever been in. There was still a medical examining table with all the accoutrements. There were maps of the human bodies' various structures: nervous, skeletal, and circulatory. No photos of Freud or Einstein, which always seemed to adorn the walls in Tom's imagination or an evening program, sitcom or drama.

On the drive over he played out a whole conversation with the doctor in his head:

"Tell me about your mother. Do you love her?" And he even had a Freudian accent. Or one that Tom imagined Freud having.

"Of course, she's my mother."

"Did you have a long attachment with her? Let's say, nursing?"

"What? No! I don't think so. I mean, I don't remember it…."

"Hmmm."

"What are you trying to say, here?"

"Why did they call you Tommy Titsucker in school?"

"What?"

"Everyone has a sexual attachment to one's mother."

"Get out of here."

"After all, she was the first woman to ever spread her legs for you."

There was none of that. The ensuing session or interview was not what Tom imagined. Mostly the doctor asked him about his sleeping and eating habits and looked him over a bit. It felt like being at the regular doctors, except with more conversation and questionnaires.

"Tell me what happened on the highway the other night, Tom," the doctor said.

"Nothing much to tell." Tom felt flush.

The doctor shrugged and held his arms in this position as though he had been frozen that way. And would he ever be back to normal? "There must be some story to tell," the doctor said, "Otherwise why would Officer Coxcomb suggest you come talk with me?"

"I don't know, really," Tom said. "It was a mis-understanding. I was looking at my gut to see if I was getting fat."

"But you're not fat, far from it." The doctor spoke softly and let go his shoulders so he once again looked like a person, a person with a neck at least.

"I know that," Tom said. "I was hoping I was getting fat, I thought I felt a paunch."

"You would like to gain weight," the doctor seemed to assert.

"So I could feel like I fit in, maybe."

"Fit in to what? Pants? Are you are looking to gain weight to find a new wardrobe?"

"No, fit in at work," Tom said, shaking his head.

"You want to fit in at work?"

"No, I don't really care." Tom knew he had stumped the doctor. He had stumped himself. The reasonable explanation, once it came from his lips, did not sound so reasonable after all. Why had he been looking at his stomach? At that particular spot. Oh, God, does the doctor know about the billboard?

"Why at that particular spot, any reason?" the doctor said and pretended to be interested in Tom's blood pressure reading. "That's an attractive young woman."

"Look," Tom said in his sternest voice, "I know what you are getting at, and no, I was not masturbating to the billboard. I pulled over to talk on my cell phone."

"And look at your belly," the doctor added.

"Sure," Tom said. There was no use explaining; these were the basic facts. Perhaps he would have started to masturbate if he hadn't been arrested, but at the actual point of contact between Tom and the officers, Tom was not masturbating, nor thinking about doing so. Much.

"Do you think there is anything interesting about sitting on the side of the road looking at your belly button, Tom?" the doctor said.

Tom flinched visibly. "Not my belly button!" he shouted, "My belly. Now you're putting words in my mouth!"

The doctor quickly jotted something down in Tom's file and then smiled graciously. "Tom, please, let's not get excited. I've hit a nerve and you don't want to discuss that subject."

"I don't really want to talk about it anymore, either," Tom said and tried to relax. It was like talking to a child, he thought.

"So we won't talk about it anymore," the doctor agreed and still smiled. The beard had a streak of silver down the center and added a distinguished flare to the man's face, so that when he smiled it could easily elicit a smile from Tom or at least put him at ease.

"Alright," Tom said, "it is a little odd, I can see that. But it's nothing like the police are making it out to be."

"Do you often feel people are out to get you in this way?"

"What?"

"Can we talk about the lawn ornament incident?"

The gnome. "I'd rather not," Tom said. "How do you know about that?"

"Relax, relax." Calming smile again. Hmm, hmm. "There is no secret plot against you."

"Ok."

"But if you did feel that there were, how would it manifest itself?" the doctor said. "Do you think people speak to you through, I don't know, perhaps the radio?"

"People do speak through the radio," Tom said flatly.

"Really?"

"Sing too. It's radio."

"No, no." The doctor leaned forward. "What I mean to say is, do you feel that people speak to you personally and directly through the radio."

"Of course not," Tom said but felt as though he were lying. Just then, when the doctor asked him that question, Tom's mind flashed back to the night at the billboard. He had heard his name spoken through the radio. It was no accident and it was no mistake. When the good-looking officer was standing back at his car, Tom could hear the conversation between the officer and his dispatch. The good-looking officer spoke Tom's full name into his mic and dispatch repeated it back. "Tom Ryder" crackled through the officer's radio. Tom heard this, but knew that was not what the doctor had in mind at all, so he chose to say nothing about that. It would only confuse the issue. Tom felt he knew what the doctor was trying to do. Tom knew his defects, and psychosis was not one of them. High strung in high school, maybe. There were his pills for that. Depression? Over the years doctors and family had hinted this. Tom did not believe himself to be clinically depressed.

His father, after all, was depressed; his mother and Uncle would admit it without reluctance now, years after his death. He did not take a real interest in anything. It was hard to comprehend his father's depression, however; Tom remembers the man having hobbies and smiling a lot. He had friends. There was a favorite picture of his father Tom kept. His father has on a hat a la Frank Sinatra, tilted at an angle, smirking. Not the look at all a man who was depressed and had nothing to live for. A man who could have used a tan, perhaps. Maybe a membership to a gym. A fellow that might have looked good in a suit and tie; he had that smile. Or whatever kind of suit. Space suit. Why not? Why not to the moon? One of those men that knew mathematics so well, perhaps, that they knew satellites were the ultimate goal, not a trip to the moon (fly me to the moon).

Tom recalled verbatim his last conversation with his father. He was at university and he called his father on a pay phone down the hall from his dorm room. His father was drinking because Tom could hear Andre Ethier and the Deadly Snakes playing on the stereo in the background. One: His father was so house trained he would have never played his music too loud in the house, not even in the basement, Tom's mother would not stand for it. Two: Tom's mother, if she was home would have been swaying to different music upstairs, casting shadows on the things up there and would have certainly been on the phone as well. Three: his father was slurring a little and seemed talkative. Still, Tom liked his father after he had a few drinks. The man loosened up and talked to him as he did when Tom was smaller.

"How's the dorm?" His father asked for the third time. This time Tom expanded as both he and his father knew he would. Or was it the propensity for drunk people to repeat themselves? Either way it worked, and Tom told his father:

"There is this guy down the hall that's totally, like, he wants to instill laundry etiquette on, like the whole floor, maybe even the whole dorm…."

"Haha…"

"I know, right. He tells me and anyone that will listen…."

"Which isn't for probably very long."

"No, you're right. But he tells everyone 'if you have two or three loads that you need to wash, what you should do is wash one load and put it in the dryer but not wash the second set of clothes until half hour later. The washer takes 30 minutes and the dryer will run on the same coinage for 60 minutes. So, your clothes will sit in the washer for an unnecessary 30 minutes while some other fellow could have been utilizing the washer. If, at the end of the first 30 minutes, the washer is still empty you may start your second or third load, whatever the case may be. Even if the next fellow is only 1 minute behind you and puts his clothes in the washer, you both have utilized the washer, the water, and both your expenditures. If you happen to come out on the bottom of this transaction it will not matter, because the law of averages dictates that you will come out, if not on top, then at least even.' And all that shit."

"It makes sense."

"I guess."

"No, it makes sense."

"Sure, but the problem is, this guy, the guy with the etiquette capitalist theory, gets extremely angry if he sees a washer and a dryer going at the same time if he is trying to wash clothes. Especially if he finds out it's the same owner of both the clothes in the dryer and the clothes in the washer. There have been two or three occasions of vandalism and they blame this fellow, that's what I hear around the dorm. So he flips out and starts doing shit to people that won't buy into his theory."

"Which is a good theory."

"It is a good theory."

There was a long sigh.

"Why are people like that, dad?" Tom asked.

"I don't know what to tell you my son," his father slurred, and his last meaningful words to Tom were: "People are fucked."

Another memory from when Tom was eight. Four? He must have been six. It came back to him there in the psychologist's office. His father and mother in the car. Small Tom propped in the middle. No seatbelt, it was the late 80's. It was somehow different then, there were not enough pictures on the news of children like Tommy lying in the road having been flung through the window of a car. Hit by a drunk driver, which was somehow more accepted then, as well. His father and mother were joking around. They had just been to a garage sale in which, even though Tom was small he sensed his father had been humiliated, and he could sense too that his mother was disgusted by the whole affair. Yet they were trying to keep things light with barbs back and forth, and Tommy sensed the tension and the fun and sat giggling between them.

"It must be so hard to walk upright with no bloody spine," his mother said, and his father smiled and shook his head. "I mean really?"

"It was only two more dollars."

"The price said $5."

"Seller's remorse," his father said.

It was a fondue set, presumably in the family for over half a decade. Tom's father took it to the man with the cash box set up on a wooden table near the garage door. He produced his five dollars and said: "I've been looking all over for one of these."

"Oh, wow!" the man said placing his hand over the cash box and eyeing the five dollars suspiciously. "How did that get in here? This must be a mistake."

"Someone put a price on it." Tom's mother said, suddenly appearing at her husband's side, Tom felt his father stiffen a little.

"Well," the man said slowly, "the wife and I really do like the fondue. And it's been in this family for, shit, I don't know, years at least."

"Oh, well, that's too bad, we have been looking at getting a set." Tom's father placed the box holding the fondue set on the table.

The box showed many people smiling and sticking forks of meat into boiling chocolate/cheese/whatever your imagination wants! Try fruit for a fondue.

"Yeah, I know, but…" The man rubbed the back of his neck and grimaced long and hard. "Ah, hell, I tell you what. Six bucks and it's yours."

"Six bucks?"

"You know, you go down to Walmart and get this for ten times the price. That's a good set there, clean and only used a couple times really, and once by accident, so it was put away quickly. Seven dollars."

"You folded like that cheap table he had his money on," his mother said as his father guided their vehicle home.

Tom's father sighed. "Don't ever get married, Tommy," He said. "When you wake up one morning, lots of mornings, but one morning and say, 'I have no idea what I am doing with this person' that's when it truly is a fate worse than death." And his mother sniggered a little and punched him in the ribs before he finished saying it. But it was a joke that seemed to have been told before; it was very familiar. Or else so entirely fresh it was funny. A joke is always half a truth anyway and when the laughter was out, there was still the pilot light of the Truth glimmering in his eyes. You saw it. Still, when Tom was in a foul mood, he would take the picture out from the photo album, and the picture itself wasn't hard to find because it was the only picture Tom ever really looked at, not being a picture-looking-at kind of guy. When he was in these low moods his father's smile would take on a whole new look for him. It wasn't the smile of a care-free good old fellow just wanting to be your friend. No, this time it reminded Tom of leering, yearning beyond control. Perverted nearly. Looking for something you could never obtain. Tom could sometimes believe he saw drops of sweat on his father's forehead, near where the hat tipped so jauntily before. Not evil, but someone who would tell you about their interest in cars when clearly you were not interested. Too friendly, if there was such a thing. And there was. Or someone who would lose the focus in their eyes when they were talking about their dog. Perhaps someone who always mopped the floor and the slightest bit of dirt would make them lose their minds.

Then there were times when Tom looked at the picture and saw a man who didn't have a care in the world. Those were relaxing moments, in a way. Tom could see his own lift of an eyebrow in his father's grin. Sometimes Tom would tip an imaginary hat. These were the light feeling days when he would find that he was not fidgeting so much, or that people around him were smiling at him more. Or he was smiling at them more. Rare days, to be sure, but a reprieve Tom owed to his father's picture or even his memory. When he thought of his father he did not think of the failure his Uncle sometimes made him out to be. Nor was he confused by the man, as his mother claimed to be. When he thought of his father he felt something close to serenity, if there was such a thing. As though the moment he was in counted more than anything else. And the moment would never end; frozen in time just like his father's face tilting back a hat that he wasn't worried would fall from his head and get dirtied on the floor. If it did, there were other hats. A hat was a hat, there was no sentimentality towards a hat.

There was no real sentimentality over much. There was a house fire when Tom was young. He remembered his father laughing and watching from the street. He rescued the photo albums and clutched them under his arm and made asides to Tommy every few minutes; "Look at those sparks, Tommy." He said. Smiling at the sky. "It's getting hot here, Tommy," he said and nudged Tom on his chest until they were both on the street and then on the neighbour's lawn, with the neighbors standing looking, offering no sympathy, shocked by the homeowner's flippancy.

Tom's mother, however, ran around the neighborhood shrieking to anyone who would listen about their home going up in flames, and shouting, for whatever reason "I just cleaned the house, I just cleaned the house!"

Afterwards, at his Uncle's home, he listened to his mother tell him about all the things that were now gone: an antique desk from her grandfather. "Irreplaceable," she said. A wooden clock Tom's father made in the garage, his first endeavor at woodworking. "It wasn't that great a clock," his father added. "Irreplaceable," his mother went on, speaking of things Tom had never even seen; they were so special and precious. Tucked away in the attic or garage, rarely seen by even the owners, but somehow so valuable now that they were gone. His mother cried a bit and Tom's father massaged his arm until he fell asleep and woke in his Uncle's spare room, wedged between his mother and father. At once he felt ashamed because he was too old to sleep with his parents, and relieved to know he was safe and not tucked away in an attic or garage waiting to be burned and cried for.

Still his father was the one who was depressed and not quite comfortable in life, as his Uncle put it. For all his calmness and easygoing disposition, he must have had mental problems, his Uncle and his mother reasoned. And when Tom slipped into complacency or relaxed a little too much for his comfort, he felt afraid that perhaps he was like his father. Not comfortable in this world. Not cut out for this life. Or this race, however his Uncle always phrased it.

"Tell me something about your days in grade school, or early high school." The doctor snapped Tom into the present and Tom sat stunned for a few seconds. "Did you get along well in school?" the doctor prodded.

"Well," Tom said, "I don't know what you mean."

"Did you have many friends?"

"Not really," Tom admitted.

"Were you picked on?" the doctor asked.

"No," Tom frowned, "They did call me Tommy Titsucker for some reason."

"Any reason why?"

"I don't know," Tom said, "I don't think so. You know how kids are."

"You went to college?" the doctor said, "University?"

"I did, for a while. I dropped out."

"Why is that?"

Tom shrugged. "It was a lot of money. My father died when I started, and I just wasn't interested."

"When you started, what were you interested in doing?"

"Nothing, really," Tom said, and felt a chill of sweat run down his back. He shifted in his seat. "I can't think of anything."

"Did your parents drive you toward anything?"

Did his parents drive him toward anything? His mother, sure, always driving. His Uncle always needling on about this and that: "A man is judged in this world by his ability to earn a living, and his capacity to earn the best living he can." But his father never really gave any advice of that sort. Tom remembered many talks with the man, but never any practical advice on what to do with his life. "You'll find something." His father always smiled and they would drive in silence, with his father describing the countryside, "There used to be a farm there," he would start and Tom would watch as the old farm passed, his father's story coming to life in Tom's mind about neighbors who would help each other out, and cows dying in the spring come calving time. In Tom's imagination he could hear the hissing of oil lamps at night, and the ticking of old clocks in the silence of the living rooms, silent except for the crackling of a wood stove, which provided the only heat. There would be things to do in the morning for these people, but now there was only the hissing, the ticking, the crackling and the muted shuffling to bed. His father drove him through the country until he could see the stars in the sky through the windshield and the lights of town, the traffic getting heavier and horns shouting at each other.

And arriving home to his mother ushering him quickly upstairs to his room and admonishing his father for keeping him out so late. "It was a nice drive." He could hear his father defending himself. "He's got school," his mother would shout back. "It's Friday tomorrow," his father would reason. It made sense to Tom. Obviously to no one else.

"I think they just wanted me to be happy," Tom said, not sure if what he was saying was the truth.

"Were your parents happy?" the doctor asked.

"My dad was," Tom said, and smiled. "My father was a happy man."

"Are you a happy man?"

"Sometimes," Tom said. "When I'm not doing anything I'm happy."

"Explain that, 'when you're not doing anything you're happy', can you tell me what you mean by that?"

"I don't know," Tom admitted, "I suppose when I feel obligated to do something I get, I don't know, nervous or something."

"At work?"

"Yes, but not just at work. When I come home to Eddy and…"

"Eddy is your boyfriend?"

"Girlfriend." Tom frowned.

"I'm sorry, continue."

"When I come home to Eddy and… well, if you want the truth, she's the one you should talk to."

"And why do you say that?"

"…"

"Tom? Why do you say that?"

"It's nothing. Nothing. Forget it." Tom shifted uncomfortably.

"Tom, I want to write you a prescription for some anti-depressants. Nothing to be alarmed about…"

"I'm not alarmed."

"…many people take this medication these days. I want you to try this for a few months and make an appointment to see me in, let's say, a month or two, can you do that?"

"I suppose…"

"And there is a book I want you to pick up at a bookstore, one I think will help immensely." The doctor began writing on a pad. He ripped a page off and handed it to Tom. "Give this to my receptionist and make another appointment. We'll see how things are going after that."

Tom took the slip of paper. After he booked a second visit and left, he unfolded the paper to read what the doctor had written. The top half of the paper was an illegible prescription. The bottom half was the title of a book: Choose Your Own Reality by Travis Bunk. He already owned the book and he felt like throwing the doctor's paper away. Yet, as he walked down the street and watched others pass him with their hands deep in their pockets and their eyes on the ground, he clutched the advice in his fingers and tried to blend in with the crowd.

Chapter 12

Tom decided to park a block away from Joe Williams's home. The house was mostly dark; the only lights were shining through what must have been the kitchen window. Tom approached cautiously, nearly tripping in the fresh hole where the lawn gnome once sat. He wore a toque over his face with two eyeholes cut roughly in the wool. He clawed at the mask continuously, knowing he should have bought a balaclava, but settling on what he found in his closet. The eye holes were not matched properly, and he could only truly see out of one, the other offering unnecessary exposure to his left cheek or eyebrow, depending on how he managed it. His breath came in rapid succession, which immediately condensed inside the mask, making the wool cling to his face. His tongue flicked compulsively at what he hoped was only spit.

He held the tire iron tight in his hands as if it were a railing guiding him along a treacherous route in the dark. He knew he would have to enter through the back door, and he would have to move fast. He would have to move like the night itself, dark and dangerous…

"Hello."

"Holy shit!" Tom hissed and fell backward. He sat down hard on the concrete and reflexively searched for the tire-iron while fumbling with his mask. He tilted his head back to see who was speaking. It was one of Joe's twins, his blonde hair gleaming in the dark. Tom used the crowbar to lift himself unsteadily to his feet.

"Are you cold?" the child asked, "Is that why you have a hood?"

Tom nodded slowly and looked around for an adult as much as his mask would allow. "Is your mommy home?" he asked.

"She's at wait and see."

"Wait and see?"

"No," the child frowned. "Wait and watch."

"Weight Watchers?" Tom said.

"Yes." The child's face broke into a smile. Two front teeth gone. He looked like a sick little version of his parents. Tom felt a chill.

"Do you remember me?" Tom asked. The child shook his head no. Good. "Do you think I could talk to your daddy for a second?"

"OK." The child turned, and Tom followed him to the back door. He opened the screen door and waited until he was inside, then he slipped along the side of the house just out of sight.

"Dad!" He heard from inside the house. "A guy with one eye wants to talk to you!"

From further inside the house: "What the hell are you doing out of bed? Get up there and I don't want to see your face again until morning, do you understand?" Tom heard a smack and then a prolonged wailing, which faded away as the child presumably stumbled up the stairs. He stepped back into the shadows and felt his feet slip into the flowerbeds that lined the house. Nearly losing his balance, he used the tire-iron to steady himself against the house. Then he thought about the absurdity of his plan. He had no contingency plan at all. And really, what was he planning to do? He thought he could lure Joe out of the house somehow and then crack, right on the head. That was the extent of his planning. What if Joe was to meet him face to face as he was about to now? Could he really smack a fellow right in the head with a tire iron, all the while looking into his eyes? He couldn't even hurt the second mouse he and Eddy caught in their apartment one day. They had set a trap and when he found the mouse still alive and twitching in pain he threw up, causing Eddy to curse him and kill the mouse herself. Maybe he should have brought her. How would he explain his logic, though? He could hear the words coming out of his mouth: I am going to kidnap a man so that his family will become afraid and buy life insurance from me. It sounded so reasonable in his head when he sat beneath the image of Rebecca on the billboard.

"Hello?" Tom heard Joe coming toward the door. "Who the hell is out there?"

Tom saw Joe's bald, red face protrude from the door while the man held the screen door open. He looked first left, toward the porch light and before he could turn Tom's way, Tom placed the end of the tire iron against the folds of the man's neck. "Don't move," Tom said and heard his voice take on a decidedly Clint Eastwood vibe, straight from the Good the Bad and the Ugly. He felt a surge of excitement in his chest as he felt time stop for a second and electricity surround them both. "Don't do anything stupid, now." He wanted to say: 'do you feel lucky, punk?' but it was the wrong genre. He had already discarded using the Clint Eastwood.

"Whoa, buddy, what the hell?" Joe was holding the screen door tight and Tom could sense the man tensing.

"I mean it, I will blow your head off," Tom growled. He hoped he growled. "Just step outside and keep looking the other way. Don't you look at me." But that wasn't right. That was Dennis Hopper. No matter, it still sounded intimidating in his own ears, so how would it sound to a man with a gun/tire-iron stuck in his neck?

"Don't hurt my kids." Joe said in a low voice.

"If I wanted to hurt your kids I would have already," Tom hissed. "Why the hell aren't they in bed? It's like ten o'clock."

"I sent them to bed. The little buggers won't stay there."

"Do you read to them, motherfucker?" Tom jabbed the barrel/tire-iron forcing Joe's head to the side. "You have to read to kids."

"Sometimes I do…"

"Shut up!" Tom shouted. "Keep your head still."

"Dad?" A muffled call from the upstairs window. One of the twins was still awake; the shouting must have aroused him. Tom pushed the iron further into Joe's neck; a 'you know what to do' gesture.

"It's all right, son," Joe called out. "I'll be right up to read you a story."

"What the fuck, man!" Tom said, feeling his bladder threaten to lose control.

"Well, you said…"

"You're not going to be right up! You are being kidnapped."

"Kidnapped?" Joe tried to turn his head and stopped short. "What the hell for?"

"Just shut up." Tom fumbled with his mask with one hand until he had it off, and then fumbled again with one hand until he had it backwards on Joe's head so the eyeholes bulged with red hair and Joe's eyes were covered with wool. "Move," he said and guided Joe down the walk and onto the pavement. Joe was gagging. "It's all wet and gross," Tom heard him say through the toque.

Doot doot. Tom opened the trunk of his car with the key remote. "Hold still," he instructed his prisoner. He pulled a green sleeping bag from the trunk and stretched it out on the sidewalk. Overhead, the streetlights gleamed on the polyester fabric. Why didn't I park in the alley, Tom thought too late. What if someone sees? Idiot. "Ok. Lay down in there."

"In where?" Joe said through the fabric, his breath coming ragged and wet. Tom knew he would never wear the toque again.

"Ok, wait." Tom laid the sleeping bag open in the bottom of the trunk and then guided Joe in, all the while keeping the gun/tire-iron on Joe's neck. Joe obliged as best as a large man could getting into the trunk of a Cobalt. "Feel around," Tom said. "You feel that sleeping bag?"

"Yeah."

"Get in it."

Tom watched the man struggle blindly until he was decently engulfed in green polyester. He reached in and zipped the remaining bag over Joe's body.

"Jesus Chri…"

Tom slammed the trunk. He looked up and down the street at the dark houses. Everyone would be in bed except for Joe's kids, Tom thought. There were no cars to be seen and the only movement was the trees letting their yellow leaves sway gently in the night breeze.

Calm. A light rain began to fall and there was not even the expected struggle coming from the trunk. Ok, Tom thought. This is it.

Each turn of a corner must be accompanied with, and well in advance, a turn signal. The appropriate wait at a four way stop. Not rushing, not forcing another driver to accelerate and stop, unsure of him/her self. In fact, sometimes even waving people through when it was clearly not their turn. Tom slowed and stopped at each traffic light with the utmost respect. Never too quickly through a yellow light, but neither too quick to stop, after all, he was not in a hurry to get anywhere, but neither was he in a hurry to make it look too obvious that he was trying to look like he was not in a hurry to get anywhere.

Painfully slow, the lights of town gradually lessened in their frequency. Soon Tom was on the road he had driven that morning in preparation. It was perfect because it ran around the outskirts into a swampy area, and he could see the billboard through the trees as he drove. It was almost like a sign. It was a sign, really, a sign with Rebecca's face. Yet more than that, it was like it was Meant To Be. Karma, or something. Ordained. If he believed in that sort of thing.

The trees started to get thick and reached out and slapped his windshield. In the dark it was more disconcerting, and Tom slowed. Had he gone too far? No, he could still see Rebecca's billboard just through the trees to the right. Which pose would she be in now, he thought, feeling his back muscles relax for the first time in hours. Glasses on or off?

Suddenly, Tom felt the wheels bounce and his jaw clamped tight. He had enough time to bite his tongue while saying "Holy thit."

And then it was over. His headlights illuminated some Birch trees and there was steam coming from the front of the car. But besides his tongue he was all right. A little blood. He put the car in reverse and stepped on the gas. The car rocked, and Tom heard the tires whining.

"Holy shit, what a dick I am." He whispered a few times before finding the courage to open his door and assess the damage. "How could I be stuck!" Tom shouted at the side of the car. It was obvious, he knew. He walked around the car. Then there was a low thump from the trunk.

Tom slipped on the mud trying to get to the trunk. He took the keys from the ignition and in his haste never thought to use the trunk release. He lost the keys in the mud twice and had to bend low so he could see the moon glisten and reflect off the bumper at anything shiny on the ground. This worked the first time, but he resigned himself to spreading his hands all over the ground until he found them the second time. He popped the trunk and the sickly glare of the sleeping bag caught him off guard. He threw up. After he calmed his mind and his stomach, he pulled at the mass until it gave way and fell to the ground.

Tom lay on the dark cocoon, his breath in rapid little clouds. The wiggling stopped beneath him and in a few seconds both their breathing were long exhales. "I'm sweaty," came the resigned voice from within the sleeping bag.

"I'm going to unzip it a little bit for you," Tom gasped.

"Let me breath!" The wiggling started again.

"Shut up! Shut up!" Tom elbowed the mummified figure. The movement ceased, and Tom searched for the zipper at the head of the bag. He pulled it as much as he dared and then three white, meaty looking fingers emerged like maggots coming out of larvae. The fingers scratched and pulled until a fetus like crown appeared, and then, like the spawn of hell hath no fury, the old face of his mother. But not. No. The indignant face of a middle aged, complacent man pushed beyond limits of talking.

"What the fuck!" The face bellowed. "It's you?"

"Shut up. Just shut up." Tom said, waving the tire iron over his head, the toque in his other hand. "I just found you here. And… and I am going to take you home. Wow, lucky." He tried to smile.

"Found me here like hell, you bastard." Joe was wiggling his way out of his cocoon, kicking his legs free. He looked down at his pants. "I pissed myself, you asshole!" he shouted.

"I'm sorry!" Tom shouted back in the dark. Both men were puffing small clouds and staring at each other. Joe was prone, and Tom held the tire iron as if ready to strike. "Just shut up for a second."

After a second, "What do you want?" In place of fear, incredulity tempered Joe's words.

Tom suddenly felt it all hard to explain. He was caught. Kidnapping was a serious crime. There would be police. How could he explain his plan now? "I'm stuck," He said.

"Are you fucking kidding me?" Joe hollered. He pushed himself to his knees and craned his neck around to the car. He whipped his head back to Tom. "You're not stuck," he said.

"I am!" Tom said and waved the tire iron.

"For fuck sakes," Joe said. "First you need a spare tire and now stuck in a ditch. Don't you have Triple fucking A or something?"

"I told you to shut the fuck up," Tom said. Holy shit, would he really crown this guy? He didn't think so. But he had to make it look like he would. He saw the man wince and felt equal amounts of pity and power.

"Look, whoever you are, if I can..." But Tom was not moving. "If I can get you out of that ditch. If I can, without anyone knowing either of us were here tonight, would you let me go?"

"How can you get me out without no one knowing?"

"I have a winch on my truck at home," Joe said.

"Sure, like you would come back. Am I stupid?" Tom said.

"You drive the truck. Take me with you and we'll drive it back together, then." Joe was getting more excited by the second. Big fat beads of sweat glistened on his head.

"No way," Tom said. "You have to stay here."

"No problem, sure."

"In the trunk."

Eventually Joe agreed to climb back in the trunk if Tom promised to not take too long. They tested it for a few minutes to make sure that Joe could breathe all right and then Tom held the tire iron over his head as Joe tucked himself in among the spare tire. Joe handed him the keys.

"And remember," Tom said, "if I find any cops at your house, or if I come back and find you gone, I will kill your whole family."

"Oh, man, come on," Joe pleaded.

"Well, no, I wouldn't," Tom said, "but don't fucking go anywhere, ok?"

Tom walked through a field and three more desolate city blocks before he found a pizza place where he called a cab and sat down exhausted. He felt he might have dozed off while waiting. When he heard the honking he walked out to it in a haze. He sat in the back and couldn't think of an address so he said: "Just drive north on 67th for a while, I'll tell you where."

Tom laid his head back and let the streetlights play over his face until he felt sick again. He bolted up and sat staring at a pair of suspicious dark eyes. He recognized them somehow. A low voice called out to him in the car's darkness. "It's you."

"Sneaky back door?" Tom said, recognition flooding him with something that felt like relief.

"Beatleman!" Belraj was shaking his head. "What have you done?"

"What do you mean? What are you talking about?" Tom said too quickly.

"Oh my. You have. Or maybe you're doing it now?" Belraj sighed.

Tom tried to level his voice: "I don't know what the hell you're talking about." But he was shaking, and the words came out staccato and his pitch rose on the last word to sound like a panicked question.

"I told you I read you strong right off the get-go. So, you tell me what you are getting me and my taxi into." Belraj was firm.

"You're not into anything." Tom sat forward and pleaded. "You just take me somewhere and leave me there and forget we even met." Tom said and then added: "Again. Met again."

He saw Belraj's shoulders slacken and relax. Tom added, softly, "No one is going to get hurt, I promise. It's not that big a deal."

"I am not very happy," Belraj said and drove.

Tom paid in cash to a destination three blocks from Joe's house. Standing in front of the truck he wondered if he should kidnap Joe's wife at tire iron point and demand she drive him to the car. In the dark he fumbled with the keys until he found the fob, the symbols on it too hard to read from the streetlight, and too faded regardless. He pressed a button. The truck roared to life, headlights on, spotlights glowed from the top of the chrome roll bars. Tom reached frantically for the door handle, but the door was still locked. He wondered whether to start jabbing keys randomly as he scanned the house for signs of movement. No lights were coming on from inside the house, so he poked his thumb into another soft spot on the key-fob, hoping it was the unlock. The horn honked three times loudly, paused to tease Tom and then honked three more times.

Before the horn could settle into a routine, Tom found the proper buttons to shut it off and unlock the door. The truck also purred to a sleep as he tried to put it into reverse. He forgot to put the keys in the ignition before trying to drive away. Again he shifted through the keys. "Why so many fucking keys?" he whispered and then jerked a look at the house in case anyone should answer. Darkness there, still. He started the truck and backed out of the drive.

Wide truck tires for a guy who could barely drive his car. He steered too far toward the line in case the front of that long nose went over into the ditch. Then too far right when he thought he was going to drive right over oncoming cars. He serpentined back to Four-Mile Bridge. Which wasn't four miles from town, really, and it was more of a giant culvert over small creek. The kids played through the tunnel in the summer and sometimes there was enough water in the gully to have a nice swim.

Here the headlights illuminated the rails and the giant cucumber was hopping quickly to the center of the bridge. Joe's head had gotten free of the top of the sleeping bag and Tom could see in the wind how little hair the man actually had.

Tom pulled up behind Joe. Far enough away to barely scare the man, Tom thought, but Joe fell forward on the ground and was now a giant creeping green bug getting from rock to rock after a rain. Tom slipped getting out of the truck and his shadow loomed. "What the fuck, man?" he said to the huffing thing on the ground. "I said don't go anywhere."

"I didn't, I swear." The cocoon was trying to roll over and look up at Tom.

"Don't bullshit me, I saw you hopping along the road."

"I'm in the same spot, you asshole!" the man screamed. "You found me didn't you? I can see from here where you fucking left me, so obviously I didn't go anywhere."

"You tried," Tom reasoned.

"You can't blame a guy for trying," Joe spat.

"And what if someone ran over you?" Tom said and leaned down. He tried to pick Joe up by grabbing the sleeping bag, but the man was large and heavy. "What did you say you did for a living?" Tom asked.

"Up yours," Joe said.

Tom realized he would have to unzip the bag a little so Joe could push with his shoulders. Joe insisted on at least one free hand and Tom watched him carefully as they both struggled to get him on his feet. The surface of the bridge was more slippery and muddy than a half hour ago and it was raining harder. Joe stumbled on the sleeping bag and fell into Tom. His weight and inertia made Tom fall backward with him, gaining speed and only stopping when they came against the bridge railing. They were both breathing heavy, their breath clouds mingling and dissipating. "What could you possibly want?" Joe squeaked out between breaths.

"I just want to do a good job," Tom gasped.

"Doing what?" Joe screeched

"Disturbing you," Tom said.

"You're doing a fine fucking job," Joe said and pushed against Tom with his one free hand, Tom fell back and clutched at the sleeping bag to steady him. He saw Joe start to wiggle his hand loose and then take a halfhearted swing at Tom's head. Instinctively, Tom pushed on Joe as hard as he could to get the man away from him. Joe backed against the opposite railing and somersaulted over, gone in a flash of green polyester.

Later Tom would think how strange that there was no last-minute balancing and struggling to cling to each other faced with a newer common peril. One minute Joc was there, the next, gone. Sleeping bag and everything, like it was all sucked up in some blackness. It took Tom one second to realize what had happened. He held the edge of the railing as he looked down into the gully for Joe. He could see nothing beyond the bottom edge of the railing. "Oh no," he whispered into that pit.

Tom straightened and shot glances in every direction. There was nothing but trees dark against a sky with a lot of stars. So many stars. They were a good distance from town after all. Rain slapped on the surface of the bridge. Tom's breath rasped with clouds of white against overhead lights. "Shit," he said. Then shouted. "SHIT!"

He traced his hand along the railing as he walked toward the south end. He wished the railing would snag him somehow, prevent him from going further. But he had gone further all ready, hadn't he? No. This was not his fault. It was entirely an accident. He climbed down the embankment, there was a path there littered with gleaming rocks, slippery with the rain. The rocks also served as signposts for his way down; he slid to the bottom but managed to stay on his feet despite a few close calls.

The green sleeping bag no longer seemed green. In the dim light with the water and mud, it looked slick black. A newly polished hearse ready for the morning's event. Or perhaps nothing so dramatic. Perhaps just an ordinary black coroner's body bag. Which is essentially what it was. Now.

It was an accident, sure. But who would see it that way? As Tom stood over Joe's body, he realized there were a few holes in his plan. First, Joe recognized him. Which was solved now that he died, but this solution was now a bigger problem. He should have stopped right there, as soon as Joe knew who he was. He should have smiled and said, "I gotcha!" or "You're the winner to secretive 1000's client contest!" Maybe even suggested a reality television program. And let him go.

If he hadn't got stuck.

Tom's heart dropped. His car, it's stuck. Joe's monstrous truck should be idling heavily on the road above him. There had been no sound since Joe accidentally fell. The truck was no longer running. He clambered up the embankment, this time not caring if he remained on his feet or not, in fact, crawling most of the way, like a spider or a crab.

The truck was still there. The keys were in the ignition and Tom was able to start it. The mystery of why it would have shut off by itself was lying with Joe at the bottom of the gully. Tom drove slowly over the bridge and parked near the rear of his own car, half ditched and the trunk still open. He got out and closed the trunk of his small car, put its gearshift in neutral and wondered about how to operate a winch.

It was surprisingly easily, Tom found, despite tearing off his bumper before finding a better spot to secure the chain. He turned some knobs wrong, and some things didn't do anything, but he was able to make the winch spool in the tow chain he laid out. The car stuttered and sucked out of the dark ditch. He had trouble shutting the winch off and there was a moment of alarm when he believed his car would crush him. And after unhooking the chain and reeling in the remaining winch line he felt a little male ego pride and dusted his hands. He was able to reverse the pick-up across the bridge a bit quicker than before, one arm slung over the rear seat, head turned and eyes squinting at the road. He pulled the chain impatiently down the slope, stepping on the all the rocks as though they were placed just for him. He had the blueprint mapped out in his head, the logistics of getting this package out from under the bridge and to an as-yet-determined other location. He felt like a fireman. He pulled at the sleeping bag to see which end he was taking. Joe's head slid out from under the covering, split like a melon. Tom leaned aside and threw up.

Much later he half-heartedly invented a crime scene. After he winched Joe's body out of the gully, he placed the body behind the wheel of the truck. He gagged and cried until he finally wrapped the seatbelt around the body and clicked it into place. He then thought better and released the safety belt. The only moment in the whole evening that seemed to go as planned, however fresh and utterly improvised the plan may have been, was the part about pushing the truck, with Joe in the driver's seat, down the embankment to stage an accident. The truck went down at a good speed, all the way to the bottom. When Tom investigated as much as he was able, he was sure he saw Joe sticking through the front windshield, lying on the bed of the gully, oddly in the same position as when Tom found him the first time. Still wrapped in the sleeping bag and everything.

But Tom was not going down there again.

Chapter 13

The water cooler went "Glug"

"No… no… the guy is dead!"

"Do they know what happened?"

"Debbie's husband told her they're pretty sure it's a murder."

"No shit. That's something. Getting close to home."

"I recognize that name, I saw that name up on the board didn't I?"

"That Ryder guy had an appointment."

"Lucky."

"Bullshit. Ryder couldn't sell him."

"I bet he feels like shit."

"You would too if you were dead."

"No, I bet Ryder feels like shit."

"I know I would."

"I would have sold him."

"I would have too."

Glug

Tom sat on a stool at the bar down the street from the Consumer Life office. He was holding his third beer and that haunting phrase from his childhood rolled around in his head: never knew what hit him. Usually uttered as condolence. To Tom it seemed more terrifying. The worn-out rhetoric sparked in his brain and fired, ready to spill out, as if in some form of camaraderie around the water cooler, talking about someone else. "You always wonder about waking up one day not even knowing it's your last day." At least it was quick, they say. Never knew what hit him. These were not comfort words. The ones that waited, the ones that dragged out had time to know the fate that was due. The quick ones, the "lucky" ones had no notion of doom. Not only the morning of their last day, but right up to the very last second. For some reason, Tom thought of a close score in a hockey game where your team is sure to win. Yet there's no one in the dark arena but you, and you are so sure of victory every minute that you are not even watching the game. All the same, that bulky shadow is skating down the ice leisurely, bearing down on an empty net. And then... wham... the clock says 00:00 and somehow, they scored on you. Should you have been in net? Or maybe just watched closer from where you were? So those words were more an omen when Tom heard them. Never knew what hit him. Meaning, that bulk is out there passing the puck back and forth without tiring and without hurrying. He skates when he's ready whether you are paying attention or not. It will come for you, too. It will come for me, too. Just like it came for Joe. Like Tom came for Joe.

It was an accident. He welded this to his conscience. And while he was able to nearly convince himself, the weld marks were clearly visible. Even if Tom were able to absolve himself, others may not reach the same conclusion. Then, which version of the truth was stronger? Had he really done this thing? Had he killed a man? Him. Tom Ryder. Little Tommy Ryder who in the third grade still sucked his thumb. Little Tommy Titsucker, they called him. Which made him cry out of frustration. Not at being called a name, but from not understanding the link between the thumb and the tit. He sucked his fucking thumb, he thought (it still puzzled him, now) so why Tommy Tit-Sucker? Why not Tommy Thumb-Sucker…

"Tom?"

"Tit-Sucker!" Tom spat.

"I'm sorry?"

Tom realized there was someone addressing him. He went cold as though he were in his living room, watching TV and looked up through the living room window only to see someone standing there, staring at him. The man placed himself in the stool next to Tom. "Hello," the man said.

"Hi." Tom tried to look the good-looking officer in the eyes, yet his own felt so heavy and his neck did not feel strong enough to hold his head up, the grain of the bar so aesthetically appealing. "How are you?" he managed.

"How are you?" the big man said back to him. Not in a condescending way, but in a conspirator's tone. Comrades in something.

"I'm OK," Tom croaked.

"I have seen better days, too. I have seen worse, mind you." He smiled at Tom. His hair was black from beneath his hat. Black leather jacket and dress pants replaced the RCMP uniform. If this was casual dress for the officer it had the opposite effect on Tom. Tom felt anything but casual. All he could see were gleaming teeth floating above a black swaying balloon. The smile floated to face an approaching waitress. "I'll have a Kokanee and…" He pointed to Tom.

The waitress said proudly and quickly, "Quadrupled rum and Pepsi, tequila side and a Bud." She turned away with the satisfaction of having remembered such an order and pinned it on Tom as though the empty glasses in front of him were not evidence enough.

"Been here long?" the man said as the waitress lay their order before them.

"Not long," Tom lied. He sipped at his drink and felt his lips burn. The good-looking officer contemplated the label of his beer. "Thanks for the drink," Tom added quickly, wondering if should have said drinks.

"No problem." When the officer drank, Tom drank. Then lapsed into speculation whether the officer was subliminally making him drink, thereby easing him into doing and saying whatever the officer wanted to hear. He forced himself to drink at three, six, and eight-second respective intervals between the officer's drinks. Which dawned on him was even more clever of the bastard.

"I know why you're here," the good-looking officer said. He was looking at himself in the mirrors behind the bar. Squinting his eyes a little, and glancing quickly up out of the corner of his eye at his profile.

"You do?"

"I was on highway patrol and we used to get these accident scenes…" he spread his arms to show a loss of words. He kept speaking, rendering his body language a lie. "I've been around. I've seen a lot of weird ones," he said.

"Oh?"

"Sure. There was this one case where we had a body, obviously asphyxiated, but on what? Or by whom? Nothing in the autopsy, except that he drank some water before he died. Well, we analyzed the water and sure enough, it contained enough of his esophagus DNA for us to confirm that he had choked on an ice cube."

"Holy shit!" Tom said. "I didn't even know there was such a thing as esophagus DNA."

"There might not be," the officer said. "Can you imagine dying like that?"

Tom could not imagine. It would be awful. What would you do when realizing you were choking on an ice cube? Would you run to the toaster and stick your mouth over it? Run hot water down your throat? Or boiling water? Would you lose consciousness just after you had the capacity to think: "Why won't that fucking thing melt?"

"So these things sort of haunt you, and you look for every little thing to help. You had a client die recently, right? Your client is probably haunting you."

Tom thought of his client haunting him. He thought of ghosts. Rattling chains and gangly skeletons. Joe's skeleton calling to him at night from the apartment above his. He thought of headless mannequins hanging from their necks.

"My point is, you tend to watch for things out of the ordinary. And sometimes they end up being so ordinary that you miss them. Like your name coming up while investigating this thing. Coincidence, I know, but I just go there every time, you know?" He smiled.

"I suppose," Tom said.

"Of corpse you do."

"What?" Tom jolted his head up, suddenly sober. Did he just say corpse?

"I said of course you do." The smile. "It's hard when someone dies suddenly, someone that you work with. You are drinking here tonight because you feel guilty."

"Guilty?"

"What? No, I didn't say guilty, I said pity. For the family."

"Yes, of corpse," Tom said.

"Hmm?"

"Of course."

After a pause, the officer said, "It's funny though, how we keep running into each other. Go fugitive."

Go fugitive? That was a slip for go figure. A slip for sure, but not an obvious one. Not even a popular saying; why not go fish?

"And in my line of work it's good to keep close to people who knew the deceased, even a little bit. I'm glad you and I are able to talk." The good-looking officer smiled.

"I understand," Tom said and sucked at an ice cube from his glass. He spit it out, alarmed at the hazards. "I'm not much of a conversationalist tonight, though."

"It's been that kind of night. You don't have to talk. I respect that right to solitude."

Tom felt sweat on the back of his neck. Did he just say you have the right to remain silent? Tom felt the insane drunken urge to run. To smash all the glasses on the counter as a diversion and then bolt out the door. Or hammer the officer over the head with a bar stool. Yet, what if he was misreading the situation? Was he just being paranoid? What if, after nailing the officer with the barstool, the man just stood there, hurt but not in the physical sense and, instead of arresting Tom, said: "what did you do that for?"

The officer gulped the rest of his beer and slid a business card in front of Tom. "If you think of anything you might remember, give me a con."

Or: "Give me a call."

"I will," Tom said. "Thanks again for the drink."

"No parole," the officer said.

No problem? Tom looked up. The officer was looking into Tom's eyes with a confusing mixture of humour and threat. "You heard me that time." He left with a smile and Tom the bill.

$$$

After a few more drinks, there he was in the parking lot, fumbling with keys and then checking his wallet and cell phone. There he was pulling out of the pub with the windshield wipers on and the radio too fucking loud. Which to shut off first? And then peace after driving over the curb. Lights flowing over him were like seconds marking the passage of time before he was home. He took each off-ramp instinctively. As though he were in a river. Passing cars in and out like a fish struggling upstream. A salmon ready to spawn. He felt his member move thinking of Eddy waiting in bed. He would crawl in beside her warmth. He would pretend his fingers were tiny vehicles rolling over the hills of her thighs or shoulders. Speed bumps in certain streets became her ribs in his fantasy, making him go slow. Tracing his fingers down into her midsection, to her second set of ribs. She was so open then, so exposed and helpless. She would look into his eyes and he could really and truly see her face. And when he thought of crawling into her tonight, he imagined her sleepy face looking over at him in the dark. When did she start wearing glasses? And then, suddenly, no glasses. It was like a different chick, his member nudged him.

At home, there was the warmth of the lamp above the couch and the room was silent. In the dark kitchen he stumbled on boxes of cereal from the cupboards. He slipped on the cottage cheese and low-fat sour cream he liked on his potatoes. When he sat he was eye level with a neatly piled tower of weight loss milkshake boxes. Attached like a white flag of surrender was a note which read: "I am leaving you. You are an unsupportive fuck." Then he remembered. She was gone. He hadn't even bothered to remove her good-bye note.

Their closet confirmed it. Where her morose clothes used to cling to wire hangers, there was an empty space leaving, oddly, the exact amount of space for Tom's wardrobe. So he stood there, like he knew he should, waiting for the feeling of rage or betrayal. What crossed his mind instantly was the cottage cheese. He thought she threw that out.

Chapter 14

"Come on, come on." Tom whispered into the receiver. His hands fidgeted and twitched all over his desk, to the calendar, to his computer, picking at the fuzz on the armrests of his chair. Finally, he heard her voice on the other end.

"Rebecca speaking, how may I assist you?"

"Rebecca?" He hissed into the phone. Would she instinctively sense his panic, his consternation, would she clue in quickly without needing a lot of explaining? Of course she would. They were soulmates.

"Yes, hello? How may I assist you?"

"It's Tom. Tom Ryder," He said and exhaled with relief.

"Tom Ryder? I don't have anything on my desk regarding you. What is the problem?" Her voice was cool. She knows something is wrong. She is concerned, Tom thought. Some people did not know how to show concern and it scared them.

"Our plan, Rebecca," Tom said quickly. "Something went wrong. Something seriously went wrong."

"Our plan?" She sounded more distant and frightened with each passing sentence. "I don't know what you're talking about Tom. Mr. Ryder. What plan?"

"Good, good," Tom said, looking around his office in a state of sudden paranoia. "They could be listening. What was I thinking?"

Before he could add anything more he heard a roar from outside his door. There was a crash and slamming of doors. Another roar. Definitely coming from the foyer. "Holy shit, something weird is going on here, Rebecca. I'll call you tonight."

"Call me tonight? What the hell…"

"I have your number," Tom said. He stood up with the phone halfway to its cradle.

"You do not!" He heard her voice become tiny, "And I want to clear something up right now…" He hung up. See? It's all clear, don't worry he thought. We'll get through this.

He opened his door and stepped tentatively into the hall. There was some sort of commotion happening at the receptionist's desk. Tom followed the noise down the hall and stood at the corner near the water cooler. The receptionist was hiding her head in her thick hands and Wally and the recruiting manager looked as though they were squaring off in the center of the room, each man's bulk nearly taking up the whole of the foyer.

"Wally, listen to me, we'll get it straightened out," the recruiter was saying.

Wally's face was flush, and his massive chest was moving up and down hysterically. His wild bulging eyes wandered the room and rested on Tom. Tom felt his scrotum tighten. "They me$$ed up our pay!" Wally shouted at him. Pay? Tom thought quickly. Did he even have any pay coming? "Our pay!" Wally shouted at Tom again when he obviously did not get the response he was after. How should Tom respond? Indignant, perhaps. Outrage? They said they would straighten it out, though. Tom did not dare to reply. "My money!" Wally roared anew, and the recruiter flinched.

"Wally. Walter. Listen to me. There was a mistake…"

"Goddamn right there wa$!"

"The new commission structures have a few bugs, that's all. It will get straightened out before the end of the day, I am sure of it," the recruiter was saying, but his pleas fell on deaf, dumb and blind ears. Wally paced around the office, the receptionist letting out a small squeak whenever he passed close to her. He lashed out with one hand and hit the wall, a large framed picture with the word SUCCESS and inspirational sayings fell to the floor, the glass shattering. Tom heard a few office doors open and close just as quickly. It seemed most people in the office knew what was happening and chose wisely to stay away. Tom was not one of them.

"Thi$ will get $traightened out now, $am. No one me$$es with my $$$."

"Wally, just relax…"

"You relax, I $$$ my $$$. You think $$$ can $$$ $$$$$$$$ $$?"

"Wally!"

"$$$$ $$$, $$$$ $$$ $ $$$$$ $$$ $!"

"Take it easy, Wally." The recruiter now looked worried, not scared. Tom looked at Wally. The man's face was extremely red, now, unnaturally red. He was sweating openly; it ran in rivulets down the folds of his face and chest. His shirt was now soaked through.

"$$$ $$$$ $$$$$ $$$$$. $$$$? $$$$? $$$!" Wally said and then stumbled back and held on to the receptionist's desk to support himself. The receptionist gave out a final scream and leaped toward the exit, leaving her shawl and coffee where they sat. "$$$ $$$." Wally puffed. He reeled from the desk and swayed in the center of the room for a second, looking like he was going to explode, covering the walls with Wally. Then in an instant his eyes rolled to the back of his head and he pitched forward, slamming the waiting room magazine table into the floor, pages of insurance propaganda floating all around his head.

"Oh, my God!" the recruiter said, throwing himself on his star producer. "Tom, call 911."

"The police?" Tom hesitated.

"Ambulance, Tom! 911! Hurry!"

"$$$," Wally gurgled.

Tom found the receptionist's phone and desperately tried to think of the number for 911. It was listed on an information sheet taped to her computer. He punched it frantically while watching Wally's face. The man had been so torn up about his paycheck he had a heart attack, or something. Could Tom be that tore up about anything? Another failure on his part. That much passion looked so painful. Wally's thick eyelids were flickering up and down. If he died, Tom thought morbidly, the man would insist on loonies, not pennies, for his eyelids. And those heavy lids would clutch those dollars for eternity.

Chapter 15

Tom decided to tell his Uncle in person about Wally's heart attack but when he approached the pneumatic doors of the store nothing happened. He stamped on the mat under his feet, thinking the sensors were losing their contacts. He waved his arms at what he thought was the sensor at the top of the door. Still nothing. He could see shoppers inside and there were cars in the lot, so he knew the store was open. Using his hands, he pried the doors apart and, as though they needed the priming of Tom's fingers, they finally slid open sluggishly. Tom stepped inside and two things struck him immediately: One, there was no greeter at the entrance whom at one time had been omnipresent. Two, the mat beneath his feet, and indeed the whole of the floor throughout the store was soaking wet. There was not enough water to slosh around in, but enough traces for Tom to tell that there once had been. Recently, too.

Tom approached the first face he recognized, a teller ringing through groceries for a sullen faced woman. "Hi," he said.

"Hello." The cashier looked at him without emotion, but Tom saw the way she was ringing through the food items that something was the matter; her hands were shaking badly.

"I'm looking for my Uncle," he said.

"He's here in the store somewhere," she said. "$125.32," she told the customer, and Tom moved away. Stock boys were mopping the aisles and moving foodstuffs from the bottom shelves to higher locations. There were not as many customers as usual, but those there were pushing carts across slippery floors, once gleaming, now dull and wet. On his way to his Uncle's office he found Jude.

"Hi, it's me Tom, remember?"

"Who?" she said, glancing at the stock boys with their mops who were in turn glancing at her, she had obviously been giving strict orders on how to deal with whatever it was they were dealing with and they did not want to deviate from her plan. "Oh, Thomas," she said, "Isn't it horrible?"

"What happened?" Tom asked.

"The sprinkler system malfunctioned," she said.

"It did?" Tom asked.

"No!" she screeched, and held her head. "Oh my God, it's terrible."

Tom left her clutching her head in grief. Halfway down the first aisle he heard her regain some sort of composure and begin yelling at the staff again, directing the maneuvering of their mop work. He climbed the stairs to his Uncle's office and entered without knocking. After all, the gatekeeper was occupied. "Uncle?" he called into the dark room. He felt around for the light switches but gave up when he heard a pathetic and low moan coming from the corner. "Uncle? Is that you?"

"The sprinklers," the grieving voice said.

"The store is kind of a mess," Tom said, feeling along the wall until his hip ran against a desk. He paused, listening.

"A mess?" the voice said and then cackled maniacally. "Yes, it is a mess, isn't it? A terrible mess. HAHAHA." The laughter seemed to echo in the dark office and Tom felt hairs on his arms respond appropriately.

"Are you all right?"

"Fuck you," his Uncle spat. It was his Uncle, Tom knew. He had seen his Uncle spit that way.

Tom came to the edge of the desk and looked over. "What happened?"

There was an elongated sigh and then, "The sprinkler system went off last night. About 2:30 am. I got the call from the security company and I came right down."

"You've been here since yesterday morning?" Tom said.

"Yes! What the hell would you do." Emphasis on you. "Oh, it's Tom, I forgot." Another half insane chuckle. "Forget it."

"Why would the sprinkler malfunction?" Tom said and found the light switch. He flicked it on and the room filled with fluorescent light. It flickered enough so Tom's eyes did not have to accustom themselves and he could make out images easily and quickly. He found his uncle immediately. He was squatted in the corner, his knees pulled up to his chest, his hair disheveled and his tie askew. Shoelaces untied.

"Don't!" his uncle screamed. "Turn it off!" Tom flicked the lights off, but not before he realized there were tears streaming down his Uncle's face. Why did he have to see that right now, of all times? What should he say? Should he leave? How close could he get before knowing a sympathetic hug would be too weird? In the end he could only say, "Holy shit."

There was a long pause in the darkness. Then: "They didn't malfunction." It was a whisper, barely audible.

"What?" Tom asked.

"The sprinklers," his uncle said, "They didn't malfunction. There was a short in the lighting system and there was a small fire."

"Holy shit." Tom offered.

"Yes, holy shit," his uncle said. "The lights I put in the other day, I put them in wrong." He was staring into the wall, trying to think of someone to blame, perhaps. Or mad at himself for certain, knowing he was the cause.

"Oh."

"The security company called me, and I arrived before the fire department. The fire was small, but between the sprinkler system and the fire hoses the whole store was flooded."

"But why did Jude say the system malfunctioned?"

"You're joking with me, right?" Tom could see the sneer even in the darkness; it was something so familiar in his uncle's voice. "You don't let your subordinates know that you screwed up.

Everything I do must seem impervious. This way, they strive to do the same."

"So…"

"I told them all the sprinkler malfunctioned and ordered them to work cleaning it up."

"Ok."

"That's what you think," his uncle wailed. "It will take hours to wipe up the mess. The doors aren't working, and all the shopping carts are going shlosh shlosh shlosh all over the store."

"But…"

"You think you're so smart?" his uncle screamed. "People remember. They will never shop here again."

"Your store is spotless, as a rule," Tom said. "Maybe there are a lot of people around who shop here for convenience or drive a little out of their way for your service; surely they could forgive an amount of discomfort. It won't tear everything down."

"Exceptions," his uncle shouted. "There are exceptions to the rule and people remember! They will remember this day when the doors didn't work and there was water all over the place and the stock boy took a few more seconds attending to them because he was mopping." His uncle sobbed. "People expect - no, people demand a clean, well-lighted place in which to do their shopping."

"…"

"People are fussy about this sort of thing."

No, just people like you.

"What did you say?"

"I didn't say anything."

"But you were thinking it," his uncle said. "The thing you don't understand, Tommy, is that old saying: how you do some things is how you do everything." His uncle waited expectantly.

"You're right, I don't understand," Tom said.

"You don't understand!" His uncle began to cry. "Everything is ruined. All my life I have worked at keeping this store the safest and cleanest in the city. In the province. Maybe the country, I don't know. And now, gone. All in one day my reputation is in tatters."

Tom looked out over the store through the one-way mirror. Below him the store was in obvious disarray. Half the clerks whose job it was to stock the shelves were busy with the mopping and placing large placards around warning customers of potential impending disaster via wet, slippery floors. Here and there customers had stopped their shopping to ask well-meaning questions. Tom could see both the customers and the stock boys smiling and shaking their heads in disbelief. In one corner a woman with her young son was chatting amiably to a stock boy. He placed his hand on the boy's head and then to his own chest as though measuring the young fellow's recent and apparently surprising growth. In another aisle Tom witnessed an elderly customer hugging a stock boy in sympathy. By the dairy section a customer dressed in overalls was apparently explaining, through large friendly hand gestures the best way to go about cleaning up this sort of mess. The stock boy was taking it all in and nodding in agreement and appreciation.

"It can be cleaned, Uncle. You have a loyal customer base," Tom said.

"Loyal?" His uncle staggered to his feet and approached Tom menacingly. He grabbed Tom by his shirt collar and forced him to look closer. Tom gazed down into the aisles. There were as many shoppers as he ever remembered seeing there, they were making their way around the stock boys and smiling at each other as they passed. All Tom could see were the stock boys and the 'caution, wet floor' signs. And customers nodding sympathetically and moving on to their shopping. The water on the floor was contained and soon a large fan and heaters appeared at the end of each aisle. It would probably be dry in a few hours. "You see!" His uncle shrieked and reached up to remove a smudge on the glass. "They are devastated. They will never be back." He pointed out one shopper who was nodding and smiling at a cashier. "She is laughing at my entire operation," he said.

"I don't think she is laughing at you, Uncle," Tom said.

"Tommy, you wouldn't know if someone was laughing at someone or not. You can't even tell when people are laughing at you."

"What?"

"I mean, come on." His Uncle scrubbed at the smudge furiously, spreading it around. "You and this life insurance thing. You know you're too much like you father. You are not a business man."

"…"

"I mean, do you have what it takes?" His uncle stopped and looked at Tom. "Could you get this involved with something? Could you give your whole life to something like this?" He waved his arm at the window and his flooded store.

No.

"What did you say?"

"I didn't say anything," Tom said.

"You were thinking it, though." His uncle seemed to puff up a little; he let go of Tom's shirt and cleared his throat. "I'm not going to let this stop me," he said.

"Of course not," Tom said, frowning, trying to assimilate what his Uncle had just said to him.

"They won't shut me down."

"Why would they shut you down?" Tom asked, "Who is they?"

"They are the ones that want to shut you down. Everything you try to do, they try and make sure you don't succeed. Everyone is against you, Tommy. It's a fight. A Fight."

"I thought you set off the sprinklers."

"It doesn't matter," his uncle said. "This isn't over. This store will continue."

"Why wouldn't it continue?"

"Didn't you see the destruction, you tit?" His uncle waved out the window. Tom did not see.

"Everything will be all right," Tom said.

"Really?" His uncle pushed his face into Tom's with an expression of complete scorn. "And you know this for sure? You know for a fact? You have a crystal ball or one of them squiggy boards?"

"Ouija boards."

"So, you do? You and your mother and her hocus pocus and you with an Ouija ball?"

Tom felt his temper rising. He was familiar with the feeling, but never directed at anyone. Certainly not directed at anyone that he felt the need to express out loud. He felt his timidity suddenly slip away. He felt it as clearly as when he had thrown the rock through Joe's window. The gnome, rather.

"And what if it wasn't?" He pushed his uncle away. The older man stumbled back a few paces and stood blinking at his nephew. "What if you lost the whole store? So the fuck what?"

"What are you talking about?" his uncle asked. "You have no idea. You have no mind for business. Just like your father."

"My father?" Tom said flatly.

No mind at all.

"What did you say?"

"I didn't say anything." His Uncle said.

"But you were thinking it," Tom said. This much was true. His father had no sense of business. He remembered his mother and his father having an argument long after he was supposed to be in his bed. It was about his father refusing to join his Uncle in the store as assistant manager and part owner if they could come up with the necessary capital.

"I would not be happy working with my brother," his father said.

"It's an incredible opportunity," his mother would screech, and his father would shush her with an admonishing, "You'll wake up Tommy."

The same argument over and over. "You would be happy if we lived in this small house forever, just getting by."

"I would," his father would say, seriously. The smile in his voice uncharacteristically gone for that moment. "I don't see anything so wrong with that."

"You've got no vision."

"I have vision," his father said, laughing again. This would calm Tommy and he would rest his head against the staircase listening again to things he didn't quite understand. "I envision going fishing on the weekend," his father said.

"Going fishing?" his mother asked. "You don't catch fish."

"I catch plenty of fish."

"You don't bring any home."

"I don't like fish," his father said, "and neither do you."

"That's right, I don't."

"Then why would I bring any fish home?"

"Then why would you fish at all?" his mother said. "It's a waste of time."

"I don't think I understand you," his mother would say.

"I don't think I understand you," his father would say.

Tom shook his head sadly at his uncle. "Listen, I only came by today to tell you that Walter Russ had a heart attack. He's in the hospital."

"You're kidding?" His uncle's eyes widened. "Well, I knew it would happen someday, the man is so caught up in his work."

Chapter 16

It was ironic the way Tom kept the lights off. After the days without power, Tom thought he would be forever bathed in the light provided from the power company once again. The nights he wasn't at the billboard he sat in the basement apartment below the mannequins and stared at what could have been the opposite wall. He ate very little or not at all. Nothing changed. He had not been in to the office in several days and, when he honestly evaluated his situation, knew he probably wouldn't go back. The cable had been cut off and Tom was in no hurry to get it reinstalled. The last program he watched was the news and the lead story was Joe's death. It was regarded as suspicious, the newscaster said. Of course it was suspicious, Tom cursed. He tried to make it look like an accident and might have been successful if he had bothered to take Joe out of the green sleeping bag. It must have confused the police and rescue crew for a moment, Tom mused. No wonder the man ran his truck off the road, he imagined them saying, he's in a sleeping bag. Tom knew, however, that it wouldn't take them long to deduce that no one wrapped in a sleeping bag in that manner could drive at all. There must be something askew here, Tom could hear them theorizing. In fact, the police were no doubt connecting the dots at that very moment. As Tom sat in the dark, the good-looking officer was probably putting his case together. The meeting at the bar confirmed Tom's suspicions that they suspected him. At any moment Tom felt he would hear them at his door. Would they bother to knock, he wondered, or would they use a battering ram and bang the door down, shouting at him to lie on the floor and put his hands behind his back? Humiliation of all humiliations, and with Tom's luck, there would be a camera crew with them to film for an upcoming episode of COPS or To Serve and Protect or some such program. World's Dumbest Criminals?

On cue, Tom heard the handle of the front door turn once, twice and then clatter frantically. His heart jumped, and he felt his skin grow cold. There was someone at the door. So soon? Damn. What now?

"Hello?" he called from his seat. "Who is it?"

"Hello?" He heard a familiar voice from the other side of the door. "It's me," the voice said.

Tom flipped the dead bolt and opened the door slowly. There was a second when he wasn't sure what or who he was looking at. It was raining, so he first noticed stringy hair matted to what looked like a bone white skull. Then he noticed loose clothes hanging wet and heavy on a small frame. "Eddy?" he said.

"I need a place to stay, Tommy," Eddy said and took a step forward, falling into his arms. He held her in the doorway for a second and then noticed she was shivering. Afraid he would break her, he let go and backed into the living room, leading her by one painfully small hand.

"What happened?" he asked as she took refuge in the chair where she usually sat, her bony hands clutching at the quilt Tom handed her.

"My mother." She began to sob, and Tom held her and ran his fingers through her wet hair.

"I'll run you a bath," Tom whispered, and she nodded.

"Why are the lights out Tommy?" she asked. "Did you forget to pay the bill?"

"No, no," he said quickly. "Everything is fine. You stay here and I will run you a bath."

Tom turned on lights as he walked down the hall to the bathroom, the sudden illumination hurting his eyes. He plugged the tub and turned on the hot water, adjusting the cold with one hand and letting the water flow over his other. When the tub was half full he went back to Eddy in the living room. She was huddled beneath the quilt and he all but carried her down the hall, stripped her from her wet clothing and placed her gently in the tub. She sighed long when she hit the water and immediately submerged herself to her nose.

"Are you hungry?" he asked softly and his heart jumped. What a stupid thing to say to Eddy. Then he saw her nod nearly imperceptibly. "You are?" he asked.

"Yes."

"What can I get you?"

"Steak," she said flatly. "with lots of garlic bread."

"We don't have steak," he said. "Or bread. Actually, I don't think we have anything. Cottage cheese, maybe." He turned to the bathroom door to make like he was going to check the fridge, but there was no need; he knew for a fact they had no food.

"We could go out," she whispered. There may have been a tear running down her face, or it could have been the water. She was nearly submerged.

"We could." He thought of his bank account. Did he want to spend money on a steak dinner just to have her go to the bathroom and throw it all up? Then he felt badly about his insensitivity. "We could," he said again, hoping he sounded more convincing.

"I have nothing to wear," she said, and now he knew she was crying.

"It doesn't matter," he said. "You relax and I will dry your clothes. We will go out. We deserve it." He tried to sound cheerful.

"We deserve everything we get," she said and moved her arms about in the bath. She hardly made a ripple.

Tom gathered Eddy's clothes and threw them into the dryer. He took one of his own belts from the closet and guessed at where to make extra notches for Eddy's waist. He doubled his guess and notched three more with a steak knife while he waited for the dryer to finish and Eddy to be done her bath.

He checked on her after half an hour. She was floating with her eyes closed. "Eddy?" he asked tentatively.

"Yes?" she said.

"Nothing." He sighed with relief. "You looked so quiet and still, like you were… are you ready to go?"

"I'm in the bathtub." She sneered, and then smiled, "I'm sorry, Tommy. I had a rough week. I'll be out in a second."

"Alright." He retreated to the living room. With no television there was not much to do but wait for her to be done.

At a restaurant four blocks from their home, one they had never been to, Eddy told Tom everything that had happened since she left and went back to her mother's. "It was awful," she said, and Tom tried hard to think if he had ever met her mother (he had not) or even if he knew anything about the woman (he should have).

Here is everything, distilled for brevity, that Eddy told Tom over their two years together about her family that Tom should have remembered: her parents were born into money, Eddy's grandmother having started a clothing company called "Everyone Is Obsessed With This Clothing Company". The clothes catered to upper middle-class women with a penchant for the avant-garde. A multi-national conglomerate bought the company when Eddy's mother was still in high school and changed the name to "Everyone's Obsessed." An interesting sidebar: two of the waitresses in the restaurant at that moment were wearing garments from this company. One wore a pink thong with tassels and another wore a blouse with a picture of a mouse snorting cocaine. The waiter, of course was not wearing anything from this famous company, as he rarely wore underwear, but Eddy and Tom, not being omniscient had no way of knowing any of this. In fact, interestingly enough, Tom and Eddy happened to be the opposite of omniscient. While Eddy's mother never actually wore any of the clothes the company produced, she certainly lived off the proceeds, both she and her husband, Eddy's father, never had to work a day in their lives. They lived in a large house on a five-acre garden in the country where Eddy's father decided to become an alcoholic and her mother decided to collect porcelain dolls replete with doilies for dresses made to fit over medium sized empty wine bottles that her husband provided. They divorced as a matter of course, but each refused to give up the mansion. Luckily the mansion was large enough that neither of them had to move out and neither of them had to see or speak to each other ever again. Eddy swore at an early age that she did not want to share in her mother's frantic collections or her father's frantic intoxications. She refused their money as well, both of her parents thinking that the money would tie her to them. They were wrong. This was the reason why Tom had met neither of them. Still, no excuse for Tom not knowing about them; over the course of their two years together, she had told Tom all that is presented here at one time or another.

"It was awful," Eddy said after an appetizer of oysters in a heavy butter sauce ($14.95). "If dad isn't drinking, he's sleeping."

"Wow," Tom said, wondering if she was full.

"He drinks and then wanders around the yard singing all these old Neil Diamond songs," she said between mouthfuls. She sipped her gin and tonic ($6.99 each). "And then he passes out right in the garden. They have a maid and she brings him to bed. I think he's sleeping with her."

"I'm sorry."

"And mother…" Eddy said as the waiter came to the table to remove empty plates and bottles.

"Your steaks will be just a few more minutes," the waiter said, smiling at Eddy. *Where are you putting it all, young man*, the smile said. The steaks were $24.95 apiece. "Can I get you another drink?" ($6.99 X 2 because Tom needed another as well).

"And mother and her goddamn dolls," Eddy said. "Do you know they have conventions for those fucking things? They travel from all over the country to show each other their dolls slipped over these expensive wine bottles. Mother gets so upset because hers are the only wine bottles that are empty. They are the tackiest things I have ever seen."

"That's something," Tom said.

"I'm trying to tell them everything that's going on, you know, us breaking up and everything, and all they can do is drink and talk about dolls." Eddy sat back to let the waiter place their steaks in front of them. Medium rare with a side of baked potato, heavy with sour cream and butter, and two slices of tomato. "They didn't even bother to ask, or to notice…" Eddy raised one of her bony arms for Tom to inspect. "They didn't even want to know…"

"I'm sorry." Tom said ineffectually.

After three or four bites Eddy started to cry. "I think I'm going to throw up," she said.

"I know," Tom said and helped her out of her chair and led her to the washroom. He asked for the cheque and paid the bill while he waited for Eddy to purge. ($96.95 + obligatory 20% tip = approx. $116.00). "Make it $120.00," Tom winced to the waiter.

While Tom knew he shouldn't drive having had $6.99 X 3 drinks, he could not face calling a cab ($15.00 + $2.50 tip) and risk seeing Belraj. The man would see right through him and Eddy at this moment. Besides, it was only a few blocks away. Eddy could drive, he reasoned, the steaks, oysters and drinks out of her system by now.

Later, in bed, Tom let Eddy curl herself into a ball and wedge herself into his arms. He wrapped himself around her like a cocoon and felt protective. She fit so snugly. Was she back? Did he need her to be back? He thought so at this very instant.

"Do you ever think about those mannequins upstairs?" she said suddenly when he thought she was sleeping.

"Sometimes," he said. "I need to phone the landlord and see if they can't get curtains on the windows. It kind of gives me the creeps."

She was silent for a few seconds. "They have such perfect bodies, and they don't even have to think about it, ever."

"They don't have to think about it because they have no heads," Tom tried to joke, but the only response was Eddy's leveled breathing. "They're not perfect, they're plastic," he said finally.

"Maybe it's the same thing," she said. Tom sensed rather than heard her crying next to him. He could not bring himself to comfort her. He should respond to this, he knew.

Tom did not respond and in a short time he felt her body relax and her breathing settle into a rhythmic pace. She was asleep. Damn mannequins, he thought, if he could cut them all down he would.

$$$

The phone rang shrilly and woke Tom immediately. Confused, he rolled over in bed and found Eddy. She was back. Was she really back? How did he feel about this, he wondered. The phone insisted, and Eddy moaned in her sleep. Tom reached to answer before she woke. She needed sleep; she was so down the night before, despite having eaten a big meal, or maybe because of it. "Hello?" he mumbled into the wrong end of the receiver, turned it around and repeated, "Hello?"

"Tom Ryder?" The voice said.

"Yes?"

"This is Sam from Consumer Life." The recruitment manager. Tom was fired, he could feel it. He hadn't been to the office in nearly a week and had not bothered to phone in sick.

"Hello," Tom said flatly.

"Hi, I didn't wake you, did I? It's past noon." The voice was smiling. So eager to ingratiate. Tom recognized the slippery way of talking from their very first interview.

"No, no. I was just doing some… um… yard work," Tom said.

"In this rain?" the voice said, "What a trooper."

"Rain?" Tom said.

"Listen, I need you to come down to the office this afternoon. We have a board meeting at about three."

"About three?"

"Well, actually, at three," the recruitment manager said. "It is important that you be there, can you make it? I mean, you should make it. It's very important."

"Can you just fire me over the phone please?" Tom mumbled.

There was a huge laugh at the other end of the line, followed by intense coughing. When he was through, the recruitment manager said, "No one is getting fired Tom. It's about Wally."

"Is he…"

"Dead? Not Wally." Another laugh, morphed into coughing. "I smoke too much," the recruitment manager said in way of explanation or apology, "Wally is out of commish for a while, though, as you can imagine. What we need to do is up the productivity of the agents while Wally is on disability leave."

"What are you going to do?" Tom asked, suddenly frightened.

"We want to send eight agents to a sales conference downtown, you'll stay in a hotel for the weekend. No contact with the outside world, just immerse yourself in this conference." The recruitment manager was able to make this sound like a luxury holiday, but Tom was dubious.

"No contact with anyone?"

"No distractions at all," the recruitment manager said, "Believe me, you'll walk out of there a new man."

"I don't know…" Tom said.

"You will be paid." The recruitment manager leveled his voice.

Tom felt offended. Perhaps this tactic worked on some other agents, like Wally or the others, but not Tom. After all, Eddy had just returned; he should be working on his relationship. "How much?" he asked.

"That's what we need to discuss at the meeting," the recruitment manager said. "Some of the underwriting staff will be there as well."

Rebecca.

"I'm there. Three?"

"How about two-thirty?" the recruitment manager said. "It's actually at two thirty."

Tom left Eddy a note telling her he had to go to work and slipped out the door. Traffic was heavy at this hour and it took him longer than usual to reach the office. He entered the building with his head low and could not look the receptionist in the eye. He went to his own tiny office to check his messages: "You have no new messages," the mechanical voice taunted, and Tom left for the boardroom.

He sat guiltily in the corner, but no one seemed to notice or care about his week-long absence. In fact, none of the agents said much of anything to each other and the management did not have a lot to say to them. Wally's condition was summed up as being fine, but his doctor insisted on a period of rest. Which meant that production would be down for as long as Wally was out of the office, hence the need to get the newer or lesser producing agents up to speed. The investment was worth it, the management told the lesser agents gathered around the table, if they could each do a tenth of what Wally did in each month, the company would see it's numbers at a respectable level and the agents themselves would see their pay skyrocket.

Their itinerary was in front of them with times and locations for the various seminars as well as confirmation numbers for the hotel. The prospect of spending the weekend in a hotel only miles from home seemed strange to Tom and probably the others as well. None of them voiced these opinions. Tom knew what his position was within the organization: precarious at best. The others here did better, Tom was sure, but they were still chosen to attend the conference. They must not be as successful as Tom first thought. Perhaps there were others who had the same doubts and fears as he. Could it be? This seminar would give them a chance to hone their skills. Up close and personal for a whole weekend with the man who wrote "Choose Your Own Reality." Not just an hour in the boardroom, a whole weekend. Perhaps with some one on one time.

Eddy was still sleeping when he arrived home later. He nudged her gently and she stirred. "Eddy?" he said, "I have to talk with you." He explained his situation with as much detail as he could while she woke by degrees.

"I don't want you to go," she said flatly, her eyes beginning to flutter like water in a stream coming against rocks.

"It's just for the weekend," he said and kissed the bone of her shoulder. "I thought we needed time apart anyway. You were gone for what, a week and a bit, a couple more days will be alright."

"It's not that; it's got nothing to do with us." Tom could sense she was choosing her words carefully, trying not to hurt his feelings. She was doing a poor job. "I just don't think I can be alone right now," she said.

"But I can't take you with me," Tom said.

"I don't want to come with you."

"Well, what then?"

"I don't want you to go." She started to cry softly. "I don't think I can be alone right now."

"There is nothing in the fridge," he offered.

"It's got nothing to do with that." She sat up suddenly, shrugging off his attempt to comfort. "You don't understand anything."

"I guess I don't," Tom said, trying to keep his voice level. Was it anger he felt, resentment? It was something. An emotion. And it felt rather good. "This is something I have to do for my career." The words felt so foreign on his tongue, he was not even sure he really meant them.

Tom left her there, crying or not, and shouted back through the walls of the apartment; "I'll leave you the car." He would take a taxi. He phoned the taxi first, inexplicably asked for Belraj and packed while he waited.

Belraj didn't recognize him as Tom climbed into the back seat. He simply said into the rearview mirror: "You know who I had in my car yesterday? Elvis Presley."

"You did not," Tom said flatly.

Belraj looked in the mirror and he smiled, "Oh, it's you. No. No, I didn't."

Chapter 17

The hotel was large and clean, and Tom walked across the expanse of the lobby with his one bag in hand toward the front desk. He had to wait in line behind a large man who was waving a newspaper. "I don't want this paper," the man was saying, or shouting, depending on which side of the desk one happened to be on. "You lay this at my door every morning when I specifically requested a different paper."

"But, sir," the helpless desk clerk said, pleading with her small eyes; she must have been only twenty or so, Tom reasoned. Through a partition behind the desk Tom could see another clerk, obviously older and probably with more seniority, glancing around the corner at the altercation, refusing to get involved. "This is the paper that we give to all our guests."

"I don't care what the other guests receive." The man was raising his voice by this time, "I want the paper I requested."

"This would mean we would have to supply your paper separate from all the other…"

"Do you speak English? I ain't talkin' about what the other guests get, I am talking about what I want. I am a paying customer. I come here regularly, you little bitch!"

At this point Tom, despite his instincts, stepped toward the man and laid a hand on his shoulder. "Calm down, now," he said.

"Get the fuck off me." The man shrugged Tom's hand the fuck off him. "I want my goddamn paper. Mine, the one I read."

"The news is the same," Tom reasoned, and out of the corner of his eye saw the gratitude in the young woman, she seemed to swell. Even the timid desk manager managed to peak around the corner further than he had before. "It's all the same news. Does it really matter?"

The man looked as though he was ready to punch either Tom or the desk clerk as he backed off a few paces. "Tomorrow morning," he said savagely, "I want the paper I requested on my front door. If not, I will rip this place apart and have your job, you little slut."

"Whoa!" Tom said, but the man had already stormed off down the hall and into the elevators, complaining to everyone he met what shitty service he was receiving at this shitty hotel and how the place would be in shitty shambles by the time he was through with it, legally speaking of course, he said. "Shit!" he reiterated.

"I have a reservation," Tom said to the clerk when the man's ranting faded up the elevator shaft. "My name is Tom Ryder. I'm with…"

"I'll handle this." The desk manager finally stepped forward and pushed his way in front of the young woman. "Do you have identification?" he requested officiously.

Later, before Tom went to his room, he scoped out the halls where the seminars would be. There was a hockey reunion in a banquet hall next to where the Consumer Life seminar would be held.

Tom studied the old photos of the players, each one smiling, exposing various missing teeth. On the opposite side of the Consumer Life meeting was a seminar called: "Honey and Vinegar: Getting what you really want through kindness." Tom recognized the picture of the lecturer as the man bitching about his paper at the front desk.

The next morning, Tom foolishly thanked the electronic wakeup call that came through his telephone. He had tossed and turned all night in crisp sheets and now stumbled around half asleep looking for his clothes in a hotel that, to him, resembled his apartment a little. He banged into walls and once picked up the wall mounted hair dryer mistaking it for the telephone as it rang the reminder wakeup call. He tied his tie around his neck and spit on his shoes to give them some sort of resemblance of polish and made his way down the stiflingly hot hotel halls to the first seminar.

There were about thirty men and women in the banquet hall. Some he recognized from the office, others must have been from another agency. He did not nod in recognition at any of his fellow agents and they did not look at him. He sat alone near the back and poured himself cup after cup of free water provided in pitchers. He looked around the room for Rebecca, but she was not there. The lights dimmed, and music played from small speakers in the corners of the room. The music was fast and meant to be inspiring, but the speakers were small and Tom could hear coughs and seat shuffling over the sound.

In time Travis Bunk, author of "Choose Your Own Reality", came out from behind a curtain. He was flanked by a young woman and an older gentleman who seemed to have no other purpose than to stand beside him and frown at the crowd.

"Welcome!" Travis Bunk shouted at them.

"Ahem," someone said.

"I am glad you are all here today," he continued undaunted, "I am glad you all have made the conscious effort to CHOOSE YOUR OWN REALITY!" His flanking staff clapped enthusiastically, not quite inspiring applause from everyone gathered around the tables. Tom clapped as well, but stopped due to being the only one.

For three hours Travis Bunk ranted and roamed the banquet hall, in turns holding his book in the air and slamming it down on various tables in front of hapless agents. Tom could see some roll their eyes, and others allow light into their eyes as readily as if they were learning the secrets of the world. Tom tried to let light into his eyes but realized he was not entirely listening to the speech. He had already heard it in the office and it began to sound stale to him now. After all, what had the disturbing concept done for his client, Joe?

"I tell you the truth," Travis Bunk shouted at the ceiling so loud even his flunkies flinched, "Your potential client is not your friend, he or she is your enemy! He or she is a child who needs to be disciplined and you are the parents who know what is best. DO NOT LISTEN TO YOUR POTENTIAL CLIENT! They do not have a clue what they are talking about."

"Excuse me?" There was a voice in the back, three seats away from Tom.

"Yes, a question?" Travis Bunk smiled and offered a hand to expose the interloper.

"What about building rapport with your prospect?" The man with the question looked uncomfortable but the request was reasonable enough that the room looked as one from him to Travis Bunk.

"Rapport," Travis Bunk said flatly and let his hands fall to his side. His partners were looking at him questioningly, and he turned to them and smiled ironically. They took the cue and grinned at the ceiling as though they were dealing with a room full of imbeciles. "He wants to build rapport," Travis Bunk said as an aside to his aides.

"Yes, rapport," The man said evenly. He did not shift uncomfortably as Tom was doing now, nor did he take his eyes off Travis Bunk; his timidity apparently gone after being singled out.

"What's your name?" Travis Bunk said and approached the man, his assistants following a step or two behind.

"Frank," Frank said.

"Well, Frank, now I know your name," Travis Bunk smiled, "Is that enough rapport?"

"It's a start."

"Where do you work?" Travis Bunk inched closer. Frank named his company and gave its address as well. "Good, good. A nice firm," Travis Bunk said.

"It is, thank you."

"How are we doing for rapport now?" Travis Bunk asked.

"Getting better," Frank said.

"Well, Frank," Travis Bunk looked to each of his cohorts, "your tie is a piece of shit."

"Excuse me?" Frank's eyes widened at the sudden attack on his wardrobe, but Tom noticed the man did not finger his tie as Tom was doing at that instant, trying to draw attention away from the garment.

"You see, Frank," Travis Bunk waved Frank off and took his place in the center of the room, "You can build rapport all you want, but in the end you are going to piss your prospect off. You spend all that time building a friendship and a relationship with a prospect only to shatter it when you tell them something they may feel uncomfortable listening to. Am I right?" Travis Bunk gestured to the room, but his wave ended with Tom. How the hell could he have known about the gnome, Tom wondered.

"I don't think you're right at all." Frank ventured, and the room sat silent.

"Oh?"

"No," Frank continued. "Your idea of disturbing is sound enough, but I think you are missing the point here."

"I'm missing the point." Travis Bunk laughed out loud at the prospect. His aides laughed as well, but Tom noticed that not many others in the room were laughing. They were looking from Frank to

Travis Bunk, as if expecting a showdown. "If you would have bothered to read my book, the reason we are all gathered here…"

"I have read your book," Frank answered. "I've read it twice and I think it's a piece of shit."

There was a hush in the room now. Tom could see Travis Bunk flush and his aides moved in their shoes as though they wanted to flee. "I'm sorry?" Travis Bunk said.

"You should be," Frank said. "What you are missing is the client's need to trust their agent. Your book suggests such a hostile view of the prospect, such an antagonistic stance that I can't believe it works at all."

"Really, Frank?" Travis Bunk was smiling but Tom could tell he was nervous, not used to being challenged in this way.

"Yes, really," Frank continued. "And, I checked up on you, you haven't done much else besides writing this book."

At this point a different aide, before unnoticed, was at Frank's side ushering the man out the door. Frank went quietly but smiled at Travis Bunk and tipped an imaginary hat. Bunk did not smile until Frank had safely left the banquet hall. "There goes a man who will never understand success," he said, to which his aides applauded so loudly that most of the auditorium felt they had to follow suit. "And there is a reason why he is now out in the hall, soon to be checked out of his beautiful suite, and you all are still in here." More applause. "Now, how many of you have really read my book?" He smiled sardonically while most of the hands in the room reached for the sky.

In the next few hours, Tom could hear nothing else but the words "my book", and he counted 77 times. When the seminar broke for the afternoon luncheon, Tom left with one certainty: Travis Bunk was full of shit. There was a second certainty that Tom would not realize until later that evening; he would not be back for the rest of the seminar.

Tom spent that evening and the next in his room watching old westerns that his father loved until he could finally understand what his father meant by "They're just good fun and never won any awards."

$$$

Eddy called him at midnight. Twice. The first time, in a sleeping stupor, he believed he would not be fooled into talking to the automated wakeup call system again and simply lifted the receiver and let it fall in its cradle. When she phoned the second time he was a little more awake and realized in fact that it wasn't morning, but still the same day. "Hello," he said groggily into the phone.

"Why did you hang up on me?" Her voice was far away and quiet.

"I'm sorry," He sat up in bed rubbing sleep from his eyes. "I thought it was the front desk."

"Can you come home?" she said.

"Eddy, you're not supposed to be calling me," he said, but could not remember why. Something about complete isolation from distraction.

"I need you to be here now," she said. He could tell she was crying. In his sleep state he became annoyed.

"I can't come home now," he said. "I'm in a seminar." Which was a lie, of course.

"You don't need the stupid goddamn seminar," she shrieked into the phone, so he had to hold it away from his ear. "I need you here, I said."

"What's wrong?" he asked, feigning concern.

"Nothing," she said. "Everything."

"Look, Eddy, I…"

"Now, I said." Full on shout.

"Hang on a minute, just a minute now," he tried to reason, "One day you're telling me you don't believe in me, or even love me, and now you need me there, like now?"

"I don't believe in you, and I don't love you," she said.

"Oh, very nice."

"But you must come home now." Her voice calmed a little, but there was still an urgency in it, and a resignation he had never heard before.

"Eddy, I'll be home on Monday morning," he said.

"Would you stop being so fucking selfish for once in your life and think of me?" She was not shouting at all now, but whispering words that sounded as though they should be shouted.

"Me?" Tom's face flushed. "Dammit, Eddy are you kidding me? Me, selfish? What about you? I am in a seminar here and you expect me to drop everything and just rush home because you demand it. What do you need, help lifting the couch out of the apartment? You're leaving me anyway. I can't believe this." Now it was Tom who was shouting. He could hear her shrink and stopped himself from feeling like an asshole.

"If you don't come home, I don't know what will happen," she said.

But Tom was too tired and too angry to hear the desperation in her voice. Her cryptic warning fell on deaf (and dumb, let's face it) ears. "What? What are you so afraid will happen?" he said, "You'll have a pizza or two?" He immediately felt ashamed at this, but his pride and anger and lack of sleep prevented him from taking it back, which he usually would have done. He had never said anything to Eddy about this sort of thing before and immediately after his shame he felt righteous and indignant.

"Fuck you," was all she said in way of a rebuttal and hung up, precluding any argument they might have had, and just when Tom was ready to get going. It had been so long since he felt anything like white anger and he was ready to unleash more, matching hers, of course.

When she hung up he felt ashamed again and vowed he would call her tomorrow. First, however, he called the front desk to cancel his wakeup call. The point was moot, anyhow; he had not attended the seminar that afternoon and he doubted he would be there in the morning.

Chapter 18

There is a shame that, while not exclusively known to alcoholics, is known best to that sort: that of drinking all night, missing work the next morning and drinking again that day to remedy the guilt. Tom was not an alcoholic, whatever other problems he may have had, but he was not above drinking in the afternoon. He waited until noon and called room service and got plastered on the house wine. The next morning, Sunday, he was sufficiently hungover and knew that hair of the dog would fix him up right, even though he gagged at the prospect. Had he kept up with the newspapers that were piled outside his hotel room door, or bothered to turn on the news at all, he would have realized going down to the hotel bar was a grave mistake, he would have known that his face was displayed for all to see on every newspaper and that every newscaster was saying his name and showing a picture of his home. Worse yet, they were playing sound bites of his voice. Had he known this, he would have not only skipped the hotel bar, but may have even skipped town.

He dressed as well as he was able and made his way down to the lobby, sweating and being careful not to pass the seminar doors and hoping he would not run into anyone from the meetings, especially the phony fucking author himself.

In the hotel lounge he had a beer and glanced up at the television mounted above the bar. The newscaster was looking grimly into the camera, "Breaking news," He said, "Shocking video confession of a brutal killer in our city."

Tom recognized his own face on the television. He glanced around the bar quickly to see if anyone else had noticed. He shrugged his shoulders a little and hid behind a bottle. He heard his tinny voice from the TV, but could not place the context. He stole glances at the screen. There was his picture, staring into the camera; where the hell did that come from? The caption beneath his photo read: Shocking taped confession made to officials just weeks before the murder!

Tom's television voice said, "I'm going to kill my girlfriend! Upstairs. That's where they hang them."

Tom remembered saying those things, but what had he meant at the time? Who had he been talking to? It was out of context. And again, his voice came squeaking out of the small television speakers, laughing this time: "I am not kidding you, I am going to kill my girlfriend."

Officials? It was the bloody Power and Gas Company. "Belraj!" Tom said out loud. The bartender looked over in his direction and Tom looked away. The newscast flipped back to the anchorperson. "Excuse me?" Tom ventured. The bartender smiled tightly. "Could I have the remote?"

The bartender slid him the remote and Tom pointed it at the television. Small green bars were filling up the bottom of the screen. The newscaster boomed: "We talked to Officer Coxcomb earlier this afternoon." Tom saw the officer on the screen, looking straight out at him and yelling: "We can't confirm any confession, but we can say that Tom Ryder is a definite person of interest."

"Turn it down!" from the back of the bar. The bartender came over to Tom and yanked the remote out of his hands. Soon, the volume was down, and the channel switched to a hockey game.

There was only one thought on Tom's mind as his heartbeat drowned out the television: *holy shit.* It was ridiculous. Out of context. Not even true, really. He had said those words but… could the power company just give away his recorded voice? Didn't he have to sign a release form or something? Perhaps they sold it to the news. But why? Surely they knew that it wasn't a real confession. He could sue. Yes, he would sue, and it would be the end of all his problems. What was it called? Slander? Defamation of character.

What character? The voice was real inside his head as if someone had seated next to him and spoken out loud. What character? Turn yourself in. "For what?" he whispered. For murder. "I didn't kill anyone," Tom said, a bit louder. He noticed the bartender looking at him. He tried to smile but the man looked away quickly. You didn't kill anyone? What about Joe Williams? "That was an accident," Tom said.

"Look, man, is there a problem?" the bartender said from the end of the bar. He threw a white towel over his shoulder and looked to Tom like he was about to bring his brawny bartender/bouncer body down to him.

"No, I'm sorry. It's been a rough week," Tom said

A rough week of murder, the voice said. "Fuck off," Tom shouted.

"Hey!" The bartender was suddenly in front of him. "I asked you if there was a problem here."

"No, I'm sorry," Tom said. "Could I get another beer?"

"I think it's time you hit the road," the bartender said, placing both hands on the counter and flexing massive forearms. A tattoo obscured by thick black hair read: Arms of Harm. Tom frowned. Why would someone put such a permanent stupid saying on his or her body? Same reason someone would murder someone, the voice countered.

"I didn't kill anyone!" Tom said into the bartender's face.

"No, you didn't," the bartender said. Yes, you did, said the voice. "But you are disturbing some of the other patrons."

Disturbing them? Tom looked around. "There's hardly anyone in here," he said.

"Look, do you want me to call the cops or are you just going to leave like I asked?" The bartender flexed.

Oh, that would be great; the voice was now managing irony. "No, no, I'm leaving," Tom said.

The bartender suddenly looked past Tom's shoulder, "Oh wow. You guys are fast. I didn't even call."

Tom turned on his stool and tried to stand. The good-looking officer and his partner, Thorpe were there and they each put a hand on Tom's shoulder and forced him back down into his seat. They each sat next to him at the bar.

"Can I get you gentlemen something?" The bartender looked confused. "I just asked this fellow to leave, but if he's a friend of yours, I can set you all up."

"It's fine," the good-looking officer said and waved his hand at the bartender. The man took the cue and disappeared to the end of the bar. He began drying glasses and putting them away, all the while glancing down the bar at Tom and the two police.

"Were you done here, Tom?" the good-looking officer asked Tom.

"I think so." Tom hoped he had said it out loud.

"Then would you mind coming for a drive with us?"

"Where?"

"I think you know where," he said. "I have something I want to show you."

"Did you see the news, Tom?" Thorpe smiled as he guided Tom out of his seat and toward the front door.

"Yes," Tom said. "No, I mean, I watched the weather."

Both officers were lagging behind Tom a bit and when he turned they both put their hands on his back indicating they wanted him to walk in front. They left the bar and the officers steered him away from his own car towards the police car. They asked if he would mind sitting in the back. "It's more comfortable," the good-looking officer said. "rather than have three of us jammed in the front seat."

"Can you tell me what's going on here?" Tom said as they closed the door, realizing there were no door handles on the inside of the police car. Already he felt a prisoner. Must not panic, he told himself and then heard the other voice in his head chuckling away as though he had told a great joke.

"I appreciate your cooperation, Tom," the good-looking officer said, "I am going to run you down to the station…"

"We," his partner suddenly interrupted.

"What?" The good-looking officer sounded genuinely shocked.

"We appreciate your cooperation and we are going to run you down to the detachment," his partner said. "You always do that, it's like I'm not even here sometimes, you just say 'I' this and 'I' that."

"Oh," the good-looking officer said. "Wow, I didn't realize."

"Well, you do," his partner said and looked out the passenger window into the darkness, his chin drooping a bit.

"Umm…" Tom ventured, "Are you putting me under arrest or something? I mean, both of you. Are both of you putting me under arrest?"

"Thank you for that," the sulking officer sulked.

The good-looking officer cleared his throat and made his voice sound once more officious. "Nothing like that, Tom. I… we just want to take you to the detachment and have you look at some pictures, that's all. Help me… help us out with one of our investigations."

"Can I call someone, then?" Tom asked tentatively, feeling out his situation.

"Who would you call?" came the deadpan answer. Sure enough, something was going on. They knew. Holy shit, now what? Play stupid, the other voice told him and then mentioned that it probably wouldn't be that hard for Tom, accented with another chuckle.

"The thing is," Tom said, trying to reduce suspicion, "I haven't been home all weekend. In fact, I haven't spoken to Eddy in two days and she's probably worried."

"Oh, I'm sure Eddy is just hanging around," the sulking cop said and then inexplicably burst into laughter. If it was an inside joke, it was only for him; Tom and the good-looking officer did not laugh.

"Why would you say something like that?" the good-looking officer admonished his partner. "What the hell would you say something like that for?"

"What?" his partner whined. "A joke."

"It's not even goddamned funny." Suddenly the good-looking officer was shouting. Tom cringed in the back seat. "It's not even funny. That's terrible."

"Just a joke," the partner complained and then turned to Tom in the back seat. "In different circumstances, wouldn't you think that was funny?"

"I don't think I heard the joke," Tom said.

"You didn't hear the joke?" The good-looking officer was now looking at Tom in the rear-view mirror. "Or you didn't get the joke?"

"Well, I heard what he said. Hanging around, sure. But I don't understand why that's a joke," Tom answered truthfully.

"OK," the good-looking officer answered calmly and shot a warning glance at his partner who sulked out the side window. "It's not a joke."

Tom rolled in the backseat with each turn. There were cages on each of the side windows and a cage separating Tom in the back from the driver and his partner in the front. There was no music radio, but there was a radio, squawking sometimes, making Tom uncomfortable in its codes. What the hell was a 10-46 or suspect is 10-45? What was he? Could it be that he was 10-46? The officers hadn't mentioned anything into the mic yet. What did they know about him? They were suspicious of Joe's death, that much was for certain. But they would have arrested him a long time ago. What pictures would they have? Did Belraj talk? No, he doubted that. Belraj seemed to be the type of man who would not go to the police first. Not with his mistrust of authority and government and history. The man felt the astronauts never went to the moon and the whole thing was a television studio creation. And never mind JFK. Jackie O shot him. She's a quick woman, Belraj said. There is no way Belraj would tell what he had seen that night. Or thought he saw. Still, was it Belraj who gave the audio recordings to the police? They were edited, certainly, taken out of context. The more Tom reasoned the more he convinced himself that his actions, while not innocuous, were still ambiguous. Start asking for a lawyer right off the get go, Tom told himself. This is what lawyers get paid to do. Do not be intimidated by anything. Do not let anything slip. Answer questions with simple answers, if at all. If you call for a lawyer right away, and one actually comes, then let the lawyer do all the talking from then on. That was the way to do it.

Tom felt unease immediately upon entering the underground garage of the police detachment. The good-looking officer opened the back door and held Tom's head so he would not smash it on the doorjamb. Their voices echoed hollowly and falsely against the concrete walls. Although Tom knew he must be guided through the doors in the direction they wanted him to go, he felt they were guiding him a bit too forcibly. Too aggressively if all they wanted was to speak with him about a few things. He should ask for a phone call right now, before things got too out of hand. Let them know he would not be pushed around. How much did they really know? Would asking for a lawyer be an admission of guilt?

They led him through a maze of cement walls and heavy doors that opened with magic and a loud buzzer when the good-looking officer looked into a mounted camera and flashed his identification. Soon Tom found himself giving personal information to a woman at a desk and was then quickly whisked into a private room with a large mirror on one wall and nothing on the other three. The good-looking officer pulled a chair out for Tom and sat opposite him, then glanced at the mirror and said: "Could you send Corporal Toole in with file 64-246?" Tom thought he heard something from behind the mirror and within a few seconds another officer joined them, placing a file folder in front of the good-looking officer

"All right, Tom," the good-looking officer said, "Do you have anything you want to say to me?"

Tom raised his eyebrows in question. Play it cool, he thought. "I don't think so?" he said, his voice rising.

"Absolutely sure?"

"I think so?" He questioned again and cursed himself for sounding guilty. He should be adamant. He should be angry: What are you doing calling me down here? Am I under arrest? And what for? Get me my lawyer you sons of bitches! "What's this all about?" he croaked.

The good-looking officer glanced at the mirror again and ran a hand through his hair, frowned and ran a hand through his hair again. He smoothed his tie. Officer Toole noticed this and complimented the tie

"Thank you, Toole," the good-looking officer said.

"Where did you get it?" the corporal asked.

"Moore's."

"Very nice."

"Thank you again." The good-looking officer motioned to the file and smoothed his tie once more. "That's all we need for now," he said, and the corporal nodded and left the room, stealing a glance at Tom. Thorpe folded his arms and took his place in the corner near the two-way mirror and stared at a space somewhere on Tom's forehead. Tom noticed and was uncomfortable. They knew something. Everyone knew something.

"Tom, I want you to see something," the good-looking officer said. "Tell me if you know anything at all about what I am about to show you."

Tom leaned forward expectantly as the good-looking officer pulled the file closer to him and opened it. There were many typewritten pages there and some photos which the good-looking officer removed from the folder and placed in front of Tom.

When he slapped the photographs in front of him, one by one, Tom wasn't sure at first what he was supposed to be looking at. It was his house, sure. Pictures taken from the street. There was the curtain-less bay window and the mannequins hanging. Three photos taken from different angles of the same thing. As though he were supposed to spot the difference in the pictures, the thing out of the ordinary. And then, there it was. One of the mannequins hanging from the ceiling was different. Somehow more slender than the rest. And with a head. Eddy? Eddy. Oh, my God, Eddy. O my sweetness omysweetnessnononono. Why. Why? Why Wally? Mom? Whywhywhy. Uncle falling down the stairs. Why so impressed with a winch truck would you die for it? Thoughts ran unconnected through his mind.

He looked up at the officer imploringly. Surely he could understand the coincidence. It was suicide. And a statement from a fucked-up mind. He knew immediately what they were thinking. But it wasn't true. It wasn't murder. Not this one.

"And this." The officer threw down a photocopy of official looking documents. The writing was small, but Tom could make out what it was. A copy of a life insurance policy worth one hundred fifty thousand dollars.

"Suicide," Tom croaked.

"Maybe, that's right." The officer leaned back in his chair and it did not creak under his weight. As if he had no substance that mattered to the world. But it mattered immensely to Tom. "But there is a clause in there about suicide. The money isn't payable to a suicide within two years of signing this contract. And your girl died, what, three days ago? It won't pay. Did you even read your own contract and do your job, you stupid fucker?"

Where was the good old boy from the bar? In retrospect, Tom preferred the misheard innuendos to the upfront accusations. Yet, Tom knew he was in trouble. He could not let these people sit here and accuse him of killing his girlfriend. He was in mourning, for the love of... He should be indignant. How dare you, he should scream. Instead, he croaked, "Lawyer?"

"Did your boyfriend have a lawyer?" Thorpe broke forward, enraged at the murderer before him.

"Boyfriend?" Tom asked.

"Thorpe," the good-looking officer said sternly. The man looked back at him, puzzled. Why the sudden shift in intensity? Gently, with the right amount of rebuff, remorse, and respect, the good-looking officer said, "That's his girlfriend."

"I'm sorry?" Thorpe leaned forward, not in apology, but in miscomprehension. He frowned and looked closely at the pictures. "That's a woman? But... whoa..." he stood back and at attention, looking hard at the ceiling, and swallowing hard at saliva. Only the good-looking officer hadn't flushed.

"As I was saying," he continued and tried to raise his voice to the previous level, "You fuck."

"I didn't hurt her, I wouldn't..."

"You are in a lot of trouble, here, Tom." The officer leaned forward. "I mean, let's leave the murders out of it. That's right, I said murders. I know I can get you on Joe Williams' sooner or later." He smiled, not unfriendly. "But you've got fraud of the highest order here, stealing a motor vehicle..."

"Tell him about the sexual harassment stuff!" Thorpe stepped forward and couldn't help looking at the photograph again, to make sure.

"Thorpe, would you please." The good-looking officer held his hand in the air, waving his partner back to the corner. Tom thought the man might stick his tongue out at him.

"What? Sexual harassment?" Tom asked.

"Against an employee at Consumer Life. Rebecca. You recognize the name?" The good-looking officer looked through his papers. "Some of these emails don't even make sense. What the hell is the billboard of my desire?"

"Where did you get those?" Tom demanded as much as he could with his voice shaking and his bowels threatening to give way at any moment.

"Well, it is actually company property. All your correspondence on company time and equipment belongs to them, legally." Thorpe put in and then, as though anticipating another stern warning stepped back to his corner.

"But we emailed each other. And we talked on the phone."

"So, you are saying it was a mutual thing?"

"Yes! I mean, whatever it was, it was mutual. It certainly wasn't…" Tom couldn't bring himself to say the words.

"It's strange, there doesn't seem to be any from her… to you." The good-looking officer looked up and into Tom's eyes.

Tom felt himself shrink under the stare. "Are you sure?" Yet there must have been something earnest in Tom's words and look, because he saw the officer, just for a second, shift his eyes.

"Is he sure?" Thorpe yelped from the corner, "Can you believe this guy?" He shook his head to the ceiling.

"Thorpe," the officer barked, "send Toole in here."

The guard lost his smirk quickly, "I'm sorry, last time. I swear." He pulled an imaginary zipper across his lips.

"No, please, send Toole in here."

"Honest, I got it. No more." The Thorpe insisted.

"For fuck sake Thorpe, send Toole in here now!" Thorpe jumped only slightly higher than Tom at this change in tone. He fumbled with the door handle and closed it behind him. Tom could hear murmuring just outside the door while the officer stared at his thumbs, reminding Tom of a gleaming, menace of a robot from sci-fi movies. The robots that are rendered useless until needed, to be re-activated to kill, kill, kill. Even the officer's hair was silver, Tom thought suddenly.

Thorpe came back in the room with Corporal Toole and the two shuffled at the door for a second, maneuvering until the Thorpe found his way out.

"Thorpe." The glowering good-looking robot cop came to life, "You stay in here."

"Oh, really, me?" Thorpe pointed at his own chest and looked back from Toole to the good-looking officer. "I thought… Oh, you want me to stay, too."

Ignoring him, the officer handed the reams of transcripts to Toole. "Look through these for anything we missed. Logs of her calling him, and of any emails sent. Get a fellow to look through her PC and his again for deleted files. Get those guys that can find things that are long gone, or something like that." He turned back to Tom. "I don't send anything to court that isn't air-tight my friend." He said, with an ironic smile.

Tom was too shaken up to be paying attention. He thought he just saw, among the papers the officer handed off to Toole, a printed copy of a picture he sent via email of his own schlong. He felt like shouting after Toole, "Look for her boobs on my PC!"

The officer looked Tom directly in the eye. Tom felt like looking away but knew it would be something a guilty man would do. And he was innocent, mostly, of what they were saying he did. He stared back with all his effort and focus.

"Look, we're alone now." The good-looking officer said and in his peripheral Tom saw Thorpe frowning. "Is there anything you want to get off your chest? Aren't you tired of carrying this around?"

"I don't know what you're talking about," Tom said as evenly as possible.

The good-looking officer sighed. "Did you hurt your girlfriend?"

"No." Tom was emphatic.

"You didn't hurt her even by accident?"

"No."

"Did you hurt Joe Williams, even by accident?"

"No. Umm… by accident? Oh. I didn't mean to." Tom heard the words as though someone else was speaking them. Thorpe leaped victoriously from his corner and shouted "Aha!" into Tom's face. This time the good-looking officer did not admonish him.

"Was that like a confession?" Tom finally asked.

The good-looking officer smiled. "Good enough for me," he said.

There was silence in the air. "Should I get a lawyer?"

"Too late, fucker, you already confessed," Thorpe snapped, and his eyes darted between Tom and the officer. Both men ignored him.

The good-looking officer nodded solemnly, "It would be a good idea," he said. "I will inform you now, Tom Ryder, that I am placing you under arrest for the homicide of Joe Williams." Tears began to well up in Tom's eyes.

He thought of Eddy. Gone. His mind wandered down the corridors of his office. Every cubicle and office emptied out. The carpet torn up and the walls whitewashed. What little furniture there was left covered in plastic. Equally, his Uncle's store drifted through his consciousness, the shelves bereft of goods, and the fluorescents above replaced by a long-lasting sort of bulb that seems to never need replacing. He thought of his mother. His mother. How would it look to her? And then, he felt an indefinable gratitude that his father was not alive. How would his father see his deeds? We help you look better. See?

Tom blinked. What the hell was a billboard of my desire, anyway? This awareness of something awry hit Tom quickly enough so he could not shake it off. What about the billboard? Why had he called it Rebecca's? Oh, disillusioned drunken fool, you have staggered around out there calling her name. Worse, no messages from Rebecca to him? Is that what this man said? There were phone calls he remembered. Or did he remember them right? Sexual harassment. Could he have been wrong about her? Perhaps he had misread her intentions in some way. How could he have been so sure about her? He had actually thought of marriage, of all things. He wanted to see her in a wedding dress.

"Do you understand what I am telling you?" the officer was saying softly.

"I do," Tom said. Or he may have just nodded.

"Ok. Is there anyone you would like to call?" the good-looking officer asked. Tom nodded, yes. "Then we'll get some of the paperwork out of the way and arrange for you to come down to the phone room, all right? About an hour?" Tom nodded. "You think of everyone you want to call, within reason, and we'll just put you in the holding cell. I don't need to put handcuffs on you, do I, Tom?" the good-looking officer asked.

The cell was sort of the way Tom imagined. Cement walls, brightly chipped yellow painted steel bunks, infamous bars, of course, and a coarse steel mesh covering those. He knew that unrolling the bedroll provided would add to the permanence, so he sat on the cot and held his hair with clenched, angry fists. It was like a whirlwind. One day, driving around, the next, locked up. Maybe forever. Where would he go? How could he survive? Could he get out of this somehow? Did he know a lawyer? His mother or Uncle would know a lawyer. But, just what the hell was he going to say to either of them? He had to phone Rebecca. She would know what to do. Yet, was she real? She was adding sexual harassment to his charges. He had to get an explanation from her. It didn't sit right with Tom. There was something wrong. They had gotten to her somehow. Sure, that made sense. In this way, she would be privy to every part of whatever they had against him. Oh, clever girl. She would be his lawyer. She would have access to absolutely every bit of evidence. Access enough to assess it for legitimacy and relevance, but also access enough for destruction if that's what it took. Of course.

Instant relief felt like a warm shower over him and he lay on his back waiting for them to come get him. He closed his eyes. The cell sounded like the gymnasium from his old high school. Every sound echoing and seeming so far away yet right next door. He worked out what he would say to her. They would have to play stupid with each other. He would tell her in detail what happened. She would take care of everything from there. There was no need for him to call anyone else. Sweet relief. Rest now. Tom did not have to kiss the ring of his mother's god nor bow to the prime ministers on his Uncle's dollar bills.

He may have slept because it seemed like seconds later an officer came to collect him for his telephone calls. The officer handed Tom three business cards of lawyers. Tom declined, and the officer tucked the cards into Tom's shirt pocket. "It's not a good idea to do these sorts of things without a lawyer," the officer said, and Tom nodded and smiled. "It won't be necessary," he answered confidently. In the phone room, the guard sat reading a magazine, having witnessed Tom as no threat to anyone, not even himself. Tom listened to the receiver ringing and ringing. Why wouldn't she be home?

Finally: "Hello?"

"Rebecca."

"Tom, what's the matter?" Her voice sounded so soft he could barely hear it. Less than a whisper. "Where are you, Tommy?"

Tommy? I am now in love. Here now, at the end of my life I fall in love. All suspicion of his beloved Rebecca fell away from him quickly in a flood of relief and tenderness. "I'm in jail, baby." The words spilled like honey from his lips. He explained the entire story to her. From the very beginning, including his ominous cab ride that suddenly sprang into his mind. Ending with Eddy and his arrest. He was vaguely aware that the guard had dropped his magazine and now sat slack jawed and occasionally glancing over his shoulder at the mirror mounted on the wall. From behind the mirror, Tom swore he heard the muffled voice of the good-looking officer, saying: "That one is even better! Did we really get all that?" There was whooping and clapping and what Tom knew from experience was an occasional high five.

"Just take it easy, baby," Rebecca's voice hummed through the phone. "I will be right down."

"I don't think they'll let you in," Tom said.

"They have no choice," she said, and her voice sounded like the hum of two different droning tones lulling him to calm.

In his cell he opened his eyes slowly. One of the far off distant sounds was different than the others. The click-clack of high heel shoes walking down the corridors, pausing to look in each of the barred rooms housing other criminals. As the footsteps approached, Tom sat up on his cot. His heart beating faster and faster until he felt sweat accumulate on his back. Within seconds the source of the sound stopped at the bars of his cell. "Tom?" The familiar soft voice spoke through the darkness and seemingly through the stone walls.

"Rebecca?" he breathed, "You're here?"

"I told you I would come," she said, and stepped forward out of the shadows. She reached up languidly with one manicured and lovely hand; bright red nails looking wet, gently pulled off her glasses. Different chick. "Oh, Tom, what have you done?"

"I did what you told me." He was too tired to shout. Too much in love to shout.

"I didn't tell you to get caught," she exclaimed.

He hung his head and closed his eyes under the admonishment. In a few seconds he heard the cell door slowly slide open, creaking against old paint and rust. Rebecca stepped inside and closed the bars behind her. Tom felt her hands in his hair, rubbing, pulling, stroking. "My poor baby," she said. He reached out blindly and grabbed her by her hips and dragged her closer to him. He buried his face in her stomach and breathed in her far-off scent. "I love you," he whispered.

"I love you, too," she said, and slid out of her clothes and lay beside Tom on the cot. They spooned and synchronized each other's breathing.

"I just wanted to do something with my life. I wanted to be a success at something." He began to cry, slow silent sobs that upset them both.

"But you did," she said. "You set out to do something. You made a plan and executed it, all by yourself."

"I'm in jail," he said, raising his voice as much as he dared. "For murder, Rebecca. I am going to jail for a long time. I don't know how to be in jail."

From the far corner of his cell, or maybe the barred vents under his cot, came the cell neighbor's harsh shouting voice: "Shut the fuck up you fucking fuck!" Tom stiffened but Rebecca's body lay inert, unaffected.

"You see?" he whispered to her, "How am I going to survive in here?"

"We can take care of that guy," she said in the dark. "And anyone else that might hurt you here."

"How?"

He lay his head down on the pillow and listened to her as she breathed instructions. Yes, that could work. Why not? And yes, if this situation came up, she instructed him to react in this way. Yes, that would work, also. Will you stay with me, he asked her. Where else would I be, she answered and tapped him lightly on the forehead. She stroked his hair and he stretched his legs out to give his cock room.

"You can teach many people in here," she said. "And they can teach you. Trust me. And me only."

"Yes," he whispered as she wrapped around him like a second skin. Until they felt as one. The secret sharer of his thoughts.

When the guard came and peered into the cell, he at first turned away in disgust. Then he rapped on the bars with his bare hands. "Ryder!" he shouted, "You can make those calls now." He waited until Tom stood up and pulled his pants on.

"I don't know who to call," he said over his shoulder to Rebecca on the cot.

"You'll think of someone," the guard and Rebecca said at the same time, neither noticing the other was there. "Why don't you call some random people out of the phone book. Tell them what happened to Joe Williams and let them know the same thing could happen to them. You could be an advocate for Consumer Life from prison." She was suddenly excited. "They would surely pay to get you out of prison if you began scaring up business for them."

"True."

"And I will find a way out of this, for us. This is fabulous," she said.

As the guard pulled Tom out of the cell, Tom looked back on his Rebecca. "What about escaping?" he asked.

"Fuck off," the guard said and reached behind his back for handcuffs. Tom submitted easily.

Rebecca whispered the words that he already knew she was going to say, the words that were in his heart and his mind all along. "Not yet," she said, "But soon. I will tell you what to do."

Note from the author

Thanks for reading my book! I hope you enjoyed it. It was a real blast to write. Please consider leaving a review at:

https://www.goodreads.com/book/show/48049375-it-s-called-disturbing

Cheers,

Buddy Roy Baldry

www.ingramcontent.com/pod-product-compliance
Lightning Source LLC
Chambersburg PA
CBHW021308190726
48288CB00003B/743